FAITHFUL
and Other Stories

ESSENTIAL PROSE SERIES 138

Canada Council
for the Arts

Conseil des Arts
du Canada

ONTARIO ARTS COUNCIL
CONSEIL DES ARTS DE L'ONTARIO
an Ontario government agency
un organisme du gouvernement de l'Ontario

Canadä

Guernica Editions Inc. acknowledges the support of the Canada Council
for the Arts and the Ontario Arts Council. The Ontario Arts Council
is an agency of the Government of Ontario.

We acknowledge the financial support of the Government of Canada.
Nous reconnaissons l'appui financier du gouvernement du Canada.

FAITHFUL
and Other Stories

Daniel Karasik

GUERNICA
EDITIONS
TORONTO • BUFFALO • LANCASTER (U.K.)
2017

Michael Mirolla, editor
David Moratto, interior and cover design
Guernica Editions Inc.
1569 Heritage Way, Oakville, (ON), Canada L6M 2Z7
2250 Military Road, Tonawanda, N.Y. 14150-6000 U.S.A.
www.guernicaeditions.com

Distributors:
University of Toronto Press Distribution,
5201 Dufferin Street, Toronto (ON), Canada M3H 5T8
Gazelle Book Services, White Cross Mills
High Town, Lancaster LA1 4XS U.K.

First edition.
Printed in Canada.

Legal Deposit — Third Quarter
Library of Congress Catalog Card Number: 2017938076
Library and Archives Canada Cataloguing in Publication

Karasik, Daniel, author
Faithful and other stories / Daniel Karasik. -- 1st edition.

(Essential prose series ; 138)
Short stories.
Issued in print and electronic formats.
ISBN 978-1-77183-168-0 (softcover).--ISBN 978-1-77183-169-7 (EPUB).
--ISBN 978-1-77183-170-3 (Kindle)

I. Title. II. Series: Essential prose series ; 138

PS8621.A6224F35 2017   C813'.6   C2017-902331- 4   C2017-902332-2

FAITHFUL
and Other Stories

Contents

~

Mine ... *1*

Witness ... *7*

Sister ... *23*

A Much Loved Teacher ... *41*

The Snake Crosses the Tracks at Midnight ... *47*

An Old Friend ... *55*

All That Flies from You ... *61*

The Baker's Apprentice ... *67*

Rhapsody ... *77*

Faithful ... *83*

Acknowledgements ... 165

About the Author ... 167

Mine

What the family does not know is that on Saul's last night he broke his silence. Emphatically. At dusk. After four days without words, my husband said, quite loudly: Were you there? He raised his head from the pillow. Yes, he said, certainly you were there. I leaned in from my bedside chair, I took his hand, you'd think I would've been shaken, wouldn't you, after so much silence, to hear his voice, but no silence can be held indefinitely, except perhaps the silence of God. I'm here, I said. My husband looked at my face, his eyes narrowed, searching. But where was my wife? he asked me. I could not think of what to say, so I said again: I'm here.

I had been married to my husband for sixty-five years. We were well suited to each other for maybe three of them, at the beginning, and then there was a period in our fifties and sixties during which a fitful reprieve was granted; we remembered why we needed each other, if not why we had loved each other. In spite of this, or perhaps the connection is stronger than I'd care to admit, our marriage was peaceful. Consistently. I had my passions, those things I longed for, to write, to travel, I suppressed them; he had no passions—is that not fair to say? about the dead, at least, may I not tell the truth?—but in the end we were temperate people. We were unimpeachably sane. My husband's late descent into madness was nothing to lament. It was the most original, most soulful hour of his life.

I never told her, said Saul, and, foolish me, I said: Who? My wife, I never told my wife. Was I curious? Certainly I had no fear of what he might confess. I knew he'd cheated. We were not in love, after a point, and he was not in town. It was raining, he said, remember? The lawn was muddy, so I lifted your skirt so it wouldn't drag. He coughed. The effort of talking exhausted him, clearly. He sat up in bed a little, leaned towards me. Clara, he whispered to me, the situation was sad, but we made a beautiful ceremony. We did, I said, because I have always liked the name Clara. And for the proper time afterwards, he said, I went to *shul* to say Mourner's Kaddish. I lit a candle. You didn't have to leave. The mistake was the result, not what caused it.

I could feel my husband's breath on my face. I wondered what Clara might have looked like. And whether their mistake had been a boy or a girl. I gave birth to two healthy children. I never, in sixty-five years of marriage, became pregnant by accident. I chose my life, it was not forced on me. And when I listened to Saul at that hour and touched him and was tender, it was a choice. Outside it began to rain. Drops rapped at the window. Saul turned his head and looked. When he looked back to me, his eyes were full of longing. Can we go? he asked. Will you take me? He pushed himself upright. Where are we going? I asked. The yard, he whispered, smiling. Let's go to the yard.

I helped him into his shoes and out of the house. The rain matted his hair into a flat white streak. He pulled me across the lawn, he opened his mouth and caught raindrops on his tongue, he said: It's not the rain! No, no, it's not the rain! It's being here with you! He put his hands on my cheeks — touch doesn't go, other things go, touch doesn't — he touched and looked at me and saw someone else. He laughed, his shoulders rattling. A pile of bones in the flood, my husband. Even if the occasion is sad, he cried out to me, even so, I am not sad, my dear. I am not sad, my Clara. Neither am I, I said to my husband. Neither was I.

Stumbling, coughing, he led me around the side of the house, by the ruined flower bed that Shayna came to tend with me years ago, by the detached garage where Mark would lift his weights when he was in high school, to the backyard, where our apple tree grew, where it still grows, half its limbs missing where they used to hang over the neighbour's property. He stopped under the apple tree and looked at me in a way I hadn't seen him look at anybody, not even the pretty nurses, in years. He pulled me down to the ground with him, it took a minute or two, but he pulled me down, and we lay in the sodden grass with our mouths wide open to the rain. He never let go of my hand. I'm so happy, he said. And he rolled over and kissed me on the mouth. He kissed me like a young man kisses. It filled me with excitement and with shame. And even then I realized how foolish I was to be ashamed, I wasn't pretending, I didn't forget that I'm no longer young, but there's the lie, there's the great lie, that youth dies, youth doesn't die, youth gets tired and goes to sleep. And why should anyone be ashamed to wake a sleeper who has slept too long and had no one's permission to absent herself from the world? I kissed him back. A chill from the wet spread through me. His bony hips dug into my stomach, like they'd done when he was a young man. Clara, he whispered, a name I'd always liked, and I thought: what difference could a name possibly make? On the night he died, my husband was a man in love. And a name should put the lie to it? And if the time was wrong, the place, even the person, I should refuse him? Clara, my husband said to me, as soon as my kids are grown — but I put a finger to his lips, I said: Shh. It's not important now. He took me in his arms, when he didn't have the strength to hold me I took him in my arms, and after a time his body began to shake, an endless shudder took him, his teeth began to chatter, I pressed him to the warmth of my body. I did not ask him if he wanted to go back inside. My husband was cold to the touch, all of him was cold, but as long as he shook I held him and pressed him to the warmth of my body.

The family has been told he died in the hospital, but they're mistaken, he died under the apple tree in our yard. When I went into the house to call the ambulance,

I had neither the strength nor the inclination to drag him with me. The men from the ambulance found me holding him in the rain. When they asked me my name I was so tempted to say someone else's. I didn't. Of course I didn't. I'm a reasonable woman, I know the difference between real and pretend. And I know that the arms that held him in the end were mine.

Witness

~

I can pinpoint the moment exactly. I was twenty years old. In the basement of my parents' house, I had just finished watching a film. I noticed it was late, according to the clock by the TV it was 2:43 AM, and I stood to make my way towards bed. And it was as I stood that I realized with a shock, for the very first time, that I might never in my life publish a novel.

As a child I'd been certain I would one day publish a novel. Every action I took, no matter how banal, was directed towards that end. When I picked my nose, or ate a bagel, and even when I was absolutely devoted to these endeavours (and who's to say the picking of one's nose and the eating of one's bagel aren't acts worthy of a reverent concentration?), still a part of me always considered how such acts supported the eventual publication of my novel. To pick my nose was to fill time until I was ready to publish. To eat my bagel was to promote my survival until then. And to "pick and eat," so to speak, assisted in the latter way as well. I wrote novels as a child, novels that were always publishable until they were written, novels most often set in the future, because the future, I thought at the age of thirteen, I could craft however I saw fit. And so it was a shock to realize palpably, for the first time, that I might never in that malleable future publish a novel.

I'll tell you what I did, shocked in my parents' basement at 2:43 AM. I went upstairs, put on my socks, put on my shoes, put on my coat, took off my shoes, went into the bathroom, peed, put on my shoes, and left the house. It was springtime, a cool spring. I walked. My parents lived, and continue to live, in the suburbs. When I was twenty I had an apartment downtown, close to the university, an apartment I shared with a roommate I knew little and liked less than that, a roommate with such terror of silence that she felt the need to fill every moment with pounding punk rock or the drone of a TV, as though noise for its own sake might provide some comfort in the absence of consoling words or anyone to say them; and each time I returned to my parents' house, the nighttime quiet struck me as almost miraculous, and I was filled with a deep, radiating joy.

It was in this condition of deep, radiating joy, tempered by my deep, radiating distress, that I set forth into my parents' neighbourhood at a trot. I walked without direction, thinking: it's so dangerous to accept the slowness of certain processes: the writing process, the publication process, the process of finding a mate or choosing an occupation. The danger, it seemed to me as I hurried on, is that you may begin to *write off* time, to *wait* in time as though only certain moments, separated by interminable periods of absence, have significance. You say: Oh well, it's only a month till then, till I'm happy, till I can leave, till I arrive—which is a betrayal of the child you were, for whom a month was without end, the child at once immortal and without any firm belief that there would be a future. And then you say, to your own surprise: Oh well, it's only a year, I can tolerate this madness, this pain, this horror, for a year, or two, or five, and then I'll be finished, I'll be ready, I'll *publish*—until one day you hear yourself say: Oh well ... it's just a life. Oh well, I won't publish a novel this year; oh well, maybe not next; and if it should never happen, if it should happen for others and not for me, if I should turn out to be no more than a spectator to the actions of other, perhaps lesser, perhaps greater persons: oh well. And I walked faster, faster, chilled by the horror in patience.

Soon I found myself in the playground of my old elementary school, where I swung on the swings. Once the futility of such swinging struck me—I was going nowhere, and slowly—I climbed into a sort of treehouse that exists in the playground, a "treehouse" though it is connected to no tree, which leads me to think I'd best call it simply a "house," though that's even further from the truth. I peered out at the neighbourhood as though I were a near-sighted sentry, unarmed and with bad balance. I was reminded of the last time I'd sought refuge in this "treehouse," five years earlier. I'd had a rough night —I'd been angry, I can't remember what about—and had fled my parents' house, ascended to the "treehouse," made sure no one was around, and cried. I hadn't cried in ages, it was as if I'd forgotten how, so this was an event of some historical significance. It felt as though I were finding my way around the strings of a long-abandoned instrument. As I descended from my perch after the crying, a gang of tough youths watched me from beneath the gazebo that faces the playground. I was nervous that some sort of confrontation would ensue, but we just stared at each other. Their gaze said: We, dissolute and scrappy, are among others. You, puffy-eyed, are alone. This is how it'll go for you always, all your life. You'll stand exposed in the brightness of streetlamps, turned to gape at the others sheltered together in the dark.

And so I sat in that familiar "treehouse," on the night when I realized for the first time that I might never publish a novel, and wondered if anyone, ideally a girl, would arrive. And behold: a big black dog appeared on the sand beneath me, wagged its tail, looked up at me, and barked. This dog, I noticed right away, had a peculiar tail: it curled forward over his rear, so that he looked like a question mark with a dog attached. When it wagged, sometimes with vigour, sometimes as though despondent, it didn't lose its shape. It always asked a question. What's more, this dog had the most arresting face I've ever in my life seen on a dog. This dog—whose name, I would learn, was Othello—had the face of a man. His eyes, deep-set, were spaced far apart, his nose protruded and jolted slightly to the right, his mouth was delicate and set in a frown, and he appeared, from where I sat, to have cheekbones.

I stared down at this excellent dog, our gazes locked. He wagged his interrogative tail. What do you want? I asked. He barked. I hopped down from my "treehouse" and wobbled. He saw me wobble; when I regained my footing, I looked at him and saw him look away, as if to spare me embarrassment. He was much shorter than me, a fact that shouldn't have come as a surprise, but did. Had he been taller I think we might have danced, provided no one were there to see us. Instead I found a stick, gauged its weight, wrenched my arm back nearly out of its socket, and brought it forward with devastating force. The dog gave chase as soon as my stick took flight. When he arrived at its landing spot, he circled around it, unsure what was expected of him. Perhaps no one had ever thrown a stick in his company before, or had thrown sticks for other reasons, reasons in which he was not implicated. Or perhaps the face he had — the face, as I've said, of a man, as much as that can be said of anyone's face — revealed a second nature in him that warred with the canine, that contained something of the human, as much as that can be said of anyone's nature. And a dog with half a man's nature could hardly be expected to know to take a stick into his mouth.

I'm embarrassed, or really overwhelmed with shame, to admit that I clapped my hands twice, a sort of "come-hither" gesture that I'd seen others in superficially similar situations perform with their dogs. Had the dog been stupid, or stupid-looking, had he possessed floppy ears and a leering grin, I wouldn't have blushed at the less dignified customs of modern dog-man relations, I would have clapped, whistled, jeered, and petted without the slightest discomfort, as I do in the company of many humans. Yet the solemnity of Othello's face made me feel that such crassness would be a disgrace, a betrayal. I walked to my stick's landing spot, by which the dog sat, puzzled. I'm sorry, I said. Let's go.

And so we set off from the playground together. How lively was the start of our voyage through the neighbourhood! We met cats, birds, a leaf that I mistook for a frog, a mailbox that Othello mistook for a bitch, and a man watering his lawn in the dark. Unnoticed, we stood across the street and watched him for fifteen minutes, mesmerized. But nothing came of it.

We approached the running track, its surface composed of small pinkish stones, in the field behind my old high school. As a teenager I had run on this track with endless optimism, not yet aware that I might never publish a novel, still convinced that it was only a matter of time before my inability to run along the track with much grace or speed would be overshadowed by the deftness of characterization, the rigour of plot, the primordial resonance of symbol and theme that would mark my sprawling, epic, but very human novels. The track stood in my memory as a place of exultation. Which made it even harder to understand what I saw when I arrived there with Othello.

A dark shape sped over the stones. I couldn't tell

what it was—too big to be a man, yet also not a machine—and neither could Othello come to any conclu-
sions, if I may judge by the way his tail beat against my
leg. We crept closer, crouched behind bushes; I got a
clearer look. It was a horse. Yes, a horse and more than that:
men, five or six of them, dangled from its flanks. One
man, the apparent leader of the group, was mounted atop
the horse, a leg on either side, his hands around the
horse's neck. The others clung to it wherever they could
find room. The horse bucked and reared; the men hung
on. They beat it—drove their fists into its sides, rammed
their elbows into its neck. I was stunned to realize that
this was happening in silence, that neither the men nor
the horse cried out. The horse faltered, rocked from side
to side, and fell. Vomit rose in my throat as I watched
the men stomp on its head.

When they had finished, and little do I know how
they decided what constituted "finished," since their aim
seemed to be not just murder but brutality itself, they
stood by the horse's corpse. Several of them lit cigarettes.
One man pulled his jacket tighter about him, zipped it
up, and shivered. The sound of his zipper's ascent cut
through the air. I could tell now that there were five
men. All of them had blood streaked on their jackets,
their faces, their hands. The leader's hands were almost
completely obscured by blood. He held them in front of
his face and stared, transfixed. Only now, for the first
time since our arrival at the track, did I hear the men's
voices, soft and low.

What were they talking about, gathered round the

carcass of the horse they'd slain? They said nothing of
the horse, that's certain. They spoke about the weather,
how it was getting a little cool out. They spoke about
their wives, their ex-wives, about their children. They
spoke about hockey and baseball, about their morning
journey to work. It seemed that many of them commut-
ed downtown: some drove, putting up with the rush-
hour gridlock, while others took the train, on which at
least you could read the morning paper, get some work
done, have a snooze. Long silences fell between them. I
couldn't tell if they were friends, if they had a history
together, but it seemed they had little to say to one another, either because they couldn't understand each other
or because everything important between them had already been said. A couple of them seemed eager to leave.
They waited for the smokers to finish smoking, which
took a little while, since two of the smokers lit fresh
cigarettes as soon as they'd finished their first ones, ob-
livious or indifferent to the others who wished to go. At
last the men descended together to the parking lot, got
into separate cars, and drove away.

When I was sure they'd gone, I scratched the dog's
ears and led him out from our hiding place. Moonlight
glinted silver off the horse's bloody flanks. This was not
what I'd been seeking, what I'd expected to find when
I'd left my parents' house at just after 2:43 AM. Why
hadn't I stayed at home, where I was safe, where I could
console myself with masturbation and sleep?

We stood by the horse's side. I could see now why
it had suffered in silence: layers of electrical tape had

been wound round its mouth. Othello shrank back, whimpering. I felt nauseous. My worries, my ambitions, my existential quandaries, once so heavy, now seemed unbearably trivial. Who cared, for fuck's sake, that I might never publish a novel? Why accomplish anything in time — publish a novel, plant a garden, have a child, have an orgasm, consequently have another child — if time had room also for such acts as Othello and I had witnessed tonight, if a human life were the canvas on which were drawn not just acts of exaltation, loving, making, but also, and with equal grandeur, with hands covered in so much blood that the skin were obscured, acts of desecration, violation, primordial loathing? Why live at all?

We lay down and didn't sleep. We were without desire, without hope. And yet I thought: though my life's strivings might lack meaning, though what I accomplish might be smeared by the horror of other people and what other people want and do, I would not leave the murdered horse alone unseen forgotten on the empty morning field, I would stand by it, or lie by it, as the case was, and feel sadness — which I could still feel; I'm grateful — and honour a creature who knew in death nothing merciful. And if that impulse was selfish, if I did it because I wanted the same to be done for me in the hour of my death, so be it. Othello dragged his tongue across the horse's head, on which the blood had now congealed. Brown flakes scattered with each lick. It was, to my mind, in his quiet refusal to let disgust debase the violated life, a gesture of compassion.

When we had lain there awhile longer and the sun

had peeked above the nearby rooftops, a long shadow fell over us. I've never been a man to ignore a shadow when one falls over me, so I looked up. A tall man stood at my side, his face hard to make out. That's my dog, he said. I felt the warmth of Othello's breath on my cheek. Othello, the man said. My canine companion lifted his head. (It was at this point, perhaps I need not mention, that I discovered his name.) I pointed to the horse and said: It wasn't me. Did anybody accuse you? said the man. We both were silent. I asked him: What should we do? He shrugged. Do what you like. And he turned and walked away. What an animal, I thought. Othello sniffed the ground, chased his tail. Our eyes met.

I watched his question mark wag as he padded after his owner. I felt the earth under my hands, under my head. The horse and its murderers had trampled the grass for wide swaths of the field: what I saw before me was a great, unbroken flatness. Longing is endless. I could hardly remember my name. What could I do? I curled up in a ball, I shut my eyes. I listened to the wind pass through the arms of barren trees.

~

I woke to find myself in what appeared to be a jail cell. Iron bars, concrete walls. Sprawled on the floor, I wondered why I was in jail, if a jail this was, and for how long I'd been here, and for how long I would remain. Beyond the iron bars was darkness. My room contained a toilet, a cot, and a great deal of dirt. Also a small window, set into one of the walls where it met the ceiling. I stumbled to my feet. The window was high above me. I jumped, trying to catch a glimpse of what lay on the other side of it. I jumped again and again. But all I saw was the window. All my jumping did was confirm that the window was there, which I'd known already, and that light came through it. It could've been daylight or a bulb. I couldn't tell.

I became aware of a faint sound I hadn't noticed before. I held my breath, strained to hear. It was the sound of the sea. The soft throb and collapse of waves on shore. I sat on the concrete floor and listened and thought of Matthew Arnold's "Dover Beach," though what coursed through and chilled me weren't any of its lines about the sea, the sea's "eternal note of sadness," say, which "Sophocles long ago heard," but its climactic plea: "Love, let us be true to one another!" This, I thought, this is prison's true privation: to be denied, indefinitely, even the chance of love — and by love to say the revelation of something worth our fidelity. Such cruelty, to bring a man within earshot of the sea and leave him alone, with no face to which he might direct the feeling those tides call up in him!

I despaired. But soon reason took hold in me. Be sensible, I told myself. What you hear couldn't possibly be the sea. Not long ago, you were in the neighbourhood where you grew up, in the field behind your old high school, near no coast. Perhaps your jailers have furnished these sounds to lull you to sleep. This is far more likely than that you've been transported, at great expense and for no reason, to a prison by the sea.

A raspy voice whispered my name. Outside my cell, on a stool in the dark hallway, sat a short, fat man, his hair all white. There were many things I wanted to ask him — I assumed he was one of my jailors — but he spoke first. Did you sleep well? he asked. I can't remember, I said. How long have I been here? Not too long. When can I leave? That's a good question, he said.

We stared at each other through the bars. A grisly thing you did, he said, a disgusting, grisly thing. What have I done? I think you know. No, really, what have I done? You tortured and killed a horse. Oh, no — it wasn't me. Then who, he asked. I described what I'd seen. Lies, he said. What need could I possibly have to kill a horse? If it wasn't you, why did we find you in the field beside it? I was sitting vigil for it, along with a dog I met. We saw no dog. The dog was taken. By whom? By the man he rightly belonged to. Lies, he said.

He stood. Don't go, I said. Are you prepared to tell me the truth now? I've told you the truth already, I was only a witness, I'm innocent. Then what were you even doing outside at such an hour? I was wandering around, I was upset. About what? I had realized for the first time, I mean viscerally, that I might never publish a novel. He frowned. I've never published a novel — should I also kill a horse? You're missing the point. Am I, he said. And he began to stalk off into the darkness. Wait! What about my phone call? Don't I get a phone call?

He stopped, turned back. He regarded me with curiosity, as though I were a breed of prisoner he hadn't encountered before. He disappeared from sight and returned with a cordless phone, which he handed to me through the bars. Make it quick, he said, you're tying up our only phone line. You're running a jail with only one phone line? No need for more than that—you're the only prisoner. And I went cold at the thought of a fathomless emptiness around me. Make your call, he said. He sat on his stool and watched me, with no pretence of disinterest or distraction. Whomever I called, he would hear every word.

I called my parents. The line rang and rang; no one picked up. Maybe it was the middle of the day and they were at work. The answering machine clicked on; I ended the call. What message could I leave? That I'd been arrested, put in jail I knew not where, for a horrific crime I couldn't comprehend? No: better they think that I'd returned to my apartment in the city, with my roommate who feared silence. It wasn't unusual for days or a week to go by when my parents wouldn't hear from me, when I'd hardly put on clothes or even leave my solitary bed. Times of desperation, though not without their own pleasure.

The guard frowned. Wouldn't you like to tell anyone you're here? I flopped onto the cot. I'm an adult, I said childishly, I'm responsible for myself. You could be here a long time. I'd never kill a horse, I said. You're making a mistake, a big mistake. I don't believe in violence, except maybe towards myself, and then only psychological violence, and I think horses are majestic, gracious creatures, or really that's not true, I have no particularly strong feelings towards them, but certainly no hostility, either. That's what they all say, he said. Really, others have said that? Could be. It disturbs me to think that when you look at my face you see the face of someone who could beat a horse to death. He was silent a long time. Finally he shook his head. I see nothing special about your face, he said. And he stood and left.

After an interval of boredom and fear, sounds of struggle erupted near my cell. Metal rattled. A young female voice cried out: Who do you think you are, motherfucker?! Followed by: What gives you the right, you cocksucking pig's tit?! Such formulations jarred me, maybe in part because I'm incapable of street eloquence myself. I stood at the bars of my cell and peered into the darkness. The sounds of struggle persisted. A jangling of keys, a heavy door swung open, shut. Movement beyond one of my cell's walls. The sound of breath drawn deeply in.

I was glad to have company, especially since my company seemed to be a girl, but she started with the profanity again—You cowardly cocksuckers! Fucking pieces of shit!—and this didn't sit well with me. I wanted, if nothing else, a little quiet. I knocked on the wall. Who's there? my neighbour cried. I'm not sure, I responded. What are you doing here? They think I killed a horse. Why would they think that? I don't know, I guess because I was sleeping near its body. And you? What do they think you did? They say I killed my little brother. He was sick. He was in the hospital for weeks. He couldn't speak. I stayed with him. I was with him when he died. When he died I said out loud: I'm going to tell everybody, just you wait and see, I'm gonna tell every-body what a brutal shitshow this is, I'm gonna publish what I've seen. She paused. I don't know exactly what I meant, she said. I was really angry.

Perhaps I fell in love. Together this stranger and I spent hours in conversation so truthful, so rich with feel-ing, it felt like we were reinventing ourselves as we spoke. I want to see you, she said finally. How, I asked. Come to the bars of your cell, press your face to them. I'm press-ing my face to the bars too: can you see me? I pressed and pressed, my cheeks and neck began to hurt; still I could see nothing. And then — a glimpse! I could see, just barely, the tip of my companion's nose. I see you! I cried. I see you! And at almost the very same instant came her cry to me, and a cry it was, with tears in her words: I see you! Oh, there you are!

Darkness fell around us. Motherfucker, said my com-panion. I stumbled back to my cot, eased myself onto it, closed my eyes. My mind reeled in the silence. Soon I be-came aware of the sound I'd heard when I'd first woken in my cell. Waves rolled in, swept back. My breath aligned with their rhythm. I rose. I moved to the wall that separ-ated me from my companion, whispered a line of verse that coursed through and chilled me, that line of Arnold's, whispered with urgency, with a faltering voice: Love, let us be true to one another! I don't think she heard me. I didn't speak to be heard. I spoke to define and sanctify what I felt.

The door to my cell creaked open. Hands seized me, pulled me to my feet. You're so light, said a raspy voice. I could make out the glint of the guard's white hair. What's going on, said my companion. Never mind, said the guard. What are you doing to him! she shouted, pounding at the wall that separated us. Go back to sleep, the guard said. He shuffled me out of my cell. Where are you taking him! she screamed. Enough, the guard said. He led me down the hallway. Love, I whispered, let us be true to one another. Please, said the guard, his voice so terribly sad. And by love to say the revelation of something worth our fidelity: let us be true to one another. Please, he whispered, please. Double doors swung open in front of us. He led me into overwhelming brightness.

When my eyes adjusted, I saw we were in a small vestibule that separated the dark hallway from what appeared, on the other side of a door, to be the outside, daylight. The guard wouldn't look me in the face. He was much older than I'd thought, ancient. He reached into his jacket pocket and removed a crumpled pile of Kleenexes, a stick of chewing gum, and a nickel. He placed these in my hands. You're free, he said. And the charges? There are no charges. But the horse? We know you didn't kill the horse. And my time? Is there no compensation for the time I've lost? No, he said.

Sister

~

From: **marinagurtz@yahoo.com**
Sent: **January-9-09 11:10:19 AM**
To: **yourmom93@hotmail.com**

Hello Tasia,

My name is Marina. I e-mail from Russia. I am your sister. This is thing I learn not long past and I want to write you. My mother and my father are your mother and your father. They are thinking I am being dead. I am not being dead, however. I learn I am your sister by that I use internet. (Please excuse me poor English, I do not make English since school.) Now, if I am not causing great fear to you, I will try to say all. Thank you your patience. This is not next to easy.

I am your sister. The year before our mother and father leave Russia with you I am fifteen years. My mother is making round stomach because you are there. Soon you will be exhaled. One day I am in wood next to house.

In wood is river, very good and fast, full with beauty in trees and sun. When I am fifteen years I am going there always to read with the book or merely to be sitting. But this day I go into wood and something happen. I can not to remember what. But when I wake up (I do not remember going sleep) I am in a white room and beside me is man who is making medicine. This man ask my name and I am saying, Marina. They ask me where I am from and I am saying the name of our village. Then I am saying: where is here? And they say me, here is Moscow. But this can not to be something true, I am thinking, Moscow is very much distance from village. And they say me, you were bring to Moscow many month in past. Man and woman find me as if sleeping near road. These man and woman think maybe I am being dead. Therefore these put me in car and bring me at Moscow, where there is good medicine the most near. And only now I am being awake. Therefore, I am very much angry. I am saying loud, where my parents are! Where my parents are! And they are saying me they do not know who are my parents because also they do not know who is me. I am saying our parents name and again the name of our village. They say me they will discover all. The man of medicine who is most talking, he is Yevgeny Gurtz, very kind man, he take his car with me to village. We ask many question. But it is new Russia and every person have great fear of falling. We learn merely this one thing, that my parents leave and go at Canada. Then I am also having this falling, but my falling is not having floors, if you understand. And therefore I have no parents and will go to special house in Moscow where there is many children with no parents. It is bad place, deep without beauty, but then I am sixteen and I can next to leave and make normal life by alone. Yevgeny Gurtz, who is good man, he help me to go to university. I am studying deep at university and after great time I am leaving to make medicine.

I will say you how I discover that you are being named Tasia, and being alive. From when internet is born I go to English places and make our parents names. I find not anything. Then I make the Google again before I leave to make medicine here in east of Russia. I see your name with a school at Toronto, then the photograph with you inside. You are looking like me. So absolute much like me, and like our parents. It could be accident but I am absolute it is not accident. The Google say you are very deep good with clarinet. (I did not know this word, therefore I seek it on internet, and voila it is thing I love, full with beauty. I am happy.) If you are asking why I do not make telephone for you, it is because I not have great money. If you are asking why write you and not our parents, it is because I am with fear.

A very big story! I hope I do not make you with fear. I am happy if you write e-mail also and tell all things of your life.

Your sister,
Marina

~

From: **yourmom93@hotmail.com**
Sent: **January-10-09 4:22:45 PM**
To: **marinagurtz@yahoo.com**

Dear Marina,
If this is some sort of sick joke I'm calling the Russian mafia to knock you off.

I don't believe your e-mail is real. Sorry. It's very convincing, good job, woohoo, but I'm not an idiot, unfortunately. Who is this I'm writing to? Is this Dustin? If this is you Dustin I'm going to kick you really hard in the ass. You stand warned.

You asked me about my life. (Just because I choose to write to you like I believe you doesn't mean I'm convinced. Like I told you, I'm not an idiot.) I'm fifteen. As you must know. I can't write to you in Russian because my parents would never speak Russian around me, they wanted me to be a normal Canadian girl and not some crude offspring of noisy Soviet jerks. So I speak just English. I understood when you wrote "voila," though, so I guess I speak some French too. I'm in the tenth grade. My birthday is in three weeks, so I'm almost sixteen. I guess you know I play the clarinet. I also draw, and write poetry. I think I'll probably be an English or music teacher when I'm older, but I might also pursue prostitution, because of a little something we learned about in Careers class called "upward mobility." Prostitutes, if they're good at their job, have much more upward mobility than teachers do. It's cool that you're a doctor (that's the word, by the way, in English you're a "doctor"). Seems

like you can save a lot of lives *while having* upward mobility if you're a doctor.

Other things … I'm actually very shy, even if I don't
write like a shy person. If we met I probably wouldn't say
much, you'd have to do most of the talking. Oh, also,
this year apparently I have breasts, and boys want to
"jump my bones." That's a good English idiom to learn,
very useful, useful in almost every situation. And "jump
bones" is also a euphemism (which is like an idiom, but
lying) for "fuck," which is usually though not always another way to say "have vaginal intercourse with." Anyway, the point is I have breasts. I haven't let anyone jump
my bones yet, though, not even Matt, my boyfriend,
who can't stop talking about it. He's seventeen and plays
the baritone saxophone in the band. Frankly, and I can
say this if you're really my sister, I don't like the way his
penis looks and I'm not sure if I want much to do with
it. Maybe you just think I'm gross now.

I guess you probably want to know about my parents, who are your parents too if you're actually my sister
though that's still unproven. They're fine. They don't really know I exist. No, they're not fine, that was a lie. They're
sad. They're sad people who argue a lot in Russian. Except
when my dad is drinking. Then he gets totally silent and
locks himself in the study and doesn't come out even to
eat. He drinks cognac. It's not bad stuff. The scotch I
wasn't such a fan of, too strong for my taste. I'm hoping
he'll switch soon to good French wine, though stealing
that might be more obvious. (Don't think I'm that kind
of girl, I'm not, I don't even do any drugs, regularly, I just

don't believe in closing myself off to experience.) Anyway, our parents are not my best friends but they let me do pretty well whatever I want so it works out okay. Our mother likes to fuss over me and my hair and my dress whenever there's some school dance or something, but when I come home at three in the morning she doesn't wait up. What were they like when you knew them?

Hmm. I see I've started writing like I believe you. Don't assume, please. I still want more proof. Until I know for sure that you're my sister, I have lots of friends I should be messaging instead of you, a complete stranger who wrote me such a bizarro e-mail. Gotta run now.

Fondest regards,
Tasia.

p.s. Write me back soon, okay?

~

From: **marinagurtz@yahoo.com**
Sent: **January-17-09 1:13:23 PM**
To: **yourmom93@hotmail.com**

My young sister Tasia,
Our mother is having a very large brown skin on her reverse. When she curves down to pick up thing that falls, her shirt comes down at neck and it is possible you see this brown skin appear very little bit. It is looking like a star. Like something has starred her.

Our father has a nose that is not straight. It is very little bent. The special thing about this nose is that it makes him to seem he is a different man if you look to him at right side and then at left. If you want to see if it is your father who comes from mill having the bag on the shoulder, to give exemplary, you must see to him from both the sides or there is danger of wrapping all your arms on a strange man who is not being your father.

Do you like this English very much? I have been getting lesson from other "doctor" (thank you this!) who work here with me and made school in Cambridge, where there are English people who must be very much brilliant speaking because they have invented the language! Yuri tells me tell you that here is bloody cold, also when he read this about your breasts (he help translate your e-mail) he want ask if you would be very happy to come to Russia. Do not have fear, even if he is serious it is serious that is like joking, merely not.

You have ask me how were our mother and father when they were at Russia. The answer is, young. Our father was liking these drinks also then, but he was not becoming this way that you say, very quiet and falling. He was loud then with laughing and singing. The people who are knowing him sometime think he is crazy, but they like him. Our mother very beautiful. (If she is not very beautiful now I am thinking I would like you not to tell me. This is important.) Our father is leader of mill, where they make flowers. Our mother is being with me when I am child, also making many things out of cloth and sticks. Following, my father is lost from job as leader of mill. He is having great fear of future, therefore he commence to be looking for a country where he can to transport us. Our mother is very round with you. I am very before disappearing.

Our parents sound now like falling people. I have confession, I am happy they are falling, because they leave me, but also I am sad because you do not sound happy. I am sorry. Maybe I change them, when I am disappearing. But they leave. Maybe they change their selves. I am sorry still.

It is good you have boyfriend! My boyfriend is making hard work at Moscow for that we buy house together, in place near to Moscow that is full with beauty. My boyfriend also is full with beauty. I will tell you, I am very much liking his penis (this is English word I knew, factually!), but when I am only fifteen years I am with fear about this thing. Also, Yuri does not know what is this word "gross," yet if it will be making you happy and animated, yes, I think you are gross.

I am hoping now you believe I am your sister, because this is true. Please write and say me all about your friends. Again, I am so glad you exist. Have health.

Love,
Marina

~

From: **yourmom93@hotmail.com**
Sent: **January-18-09 2:43:22 AM**
To: **marinagurtz@yahoo.com**

Marina,
Let me explain something. I don't have a sister. I have never had a sister. I have spent fifteen years without a sister. Or parents, really. Or friends. Really. So don't tell me about how you're my sister and the spot on my mother's back and my dad's nose. You know nothing about it. You know nothing. You're an idiot. You can't even spell. It's *flour*, not flowers. A mill makes *flour*. You can't make flowers. Unless you're God. Who doesn't exist. Which means you're not Him. You don't know me.

Fuck off, please.

Tasia.

~

From: **yourmom93@hotmail.com**
Sent: **January-20-09 1:20:06 AM**
To: **marinagurtz@yahoo.com**

Hi Marina,
I'm sorry, I can really be quite a bitch when I want to, I don't know what I'm doing. Matt broke up with me, he's sleeping with this girl in my class who's a big pothead and wears too much makeup, I can't even look at him,

he makes me puke, literally. And I don't have any friends to talk to because all my so-called friends are interested in is TV, getting drunk with boys, and how they look. I once mentioned Emily Dickinson in front of them and they all gawked at me like I'd started speaking in tongues.

Okay, that's not the thing, so I'm going to tell you something, so before Matt broke up with me we were hanging out in his room when his parents weren't home and he tried to make me sleep with him, I rammed my knee into his crotch but for a moment before that he was inside me. There. I've said it. Written it. Now somebody else will know. Good. Great. Fantastic. Fuck fuck fuck fuck fucking shitface fuck. So how can I undo that, Marina? Will you tell me how to undo that please? Why are boys such fucking soulless animals? I hate him, I hate him so much I could choke, I want to kill him, I hate him so much I can't sleep at night, I'm going to sleep with somebody else just so I can get the guy to beat him to death for me.

You better be my sister. If you're not I'm never going to get over it. Or probably even if you are. I miss you and I don't even know you at all.

Tasia.

~

From: **marinagurtz@yahoo.com**
Sent: **January-21-09 9:35:22 PM**
To: **yourmom93@hotmail.com**

Dear my Tasia,
Thank you for this message. You make me to think of much I have not think of for very long time.

I tell you this story.

I am fifteen years. I am waking in Moscow with the doctors near to me. They are telling me I am discover near to Moscow by man and woman in their car. I am discover at this place where the road become a bridge. Under this bridge there is water that moves and is being the opposite of deep. The man and woman see me flying in the water on my reverse. I am naked. My eyes are close. The doctors tell me this. Dr. Yevgeny Gurtz, he show me a picture of me, but inside. It is a baby who is not yet a baby. Yet I am not round. Therefore, they have kill it. Yes, Jenia Gurtz say, we are killing it because it make danger to you while you sleep. Also, he say, you are killing it by sleeping. I am sad, but I am alive. And therefore I am also knowing what happen to me in the wood near my house that is so full with beauty.

I have been with horror, Tasia. But there is goodness also. Jenia Gurtz visit me every day when I am at the awful house in Moscow. When he touch me, and it is not bad like this, he touch only my head, I am with fear. He do not hate me for this. He treat me like I am his daughter. When I leave the awful house I am staying at his house many days. Following, he give me job to type papers at the hospital. Following, I am going to the university. At this year I meet son of Jenia Gurtz, who is two years more than me, and his heart is large in way that is extremely possible to see. When I am twenty-one years Mitya (this his name) touch me in the first time and I am with fear. He see this and not try to touch more. But that is not what I want. I have pain, and I do not know any things, but I know that I am liking Mitya. He follow very slow and with care. If you not understand this, my boyfriend at Moscow is Mitya. It has taken much time, but I am happy now, or what I mean is I am without horror. If you ask why we not marry, being after nine years, it is because I not have money to do this and same is with Mitya.

I am sorry you are hurt by this boy. However I want you to know that horror goes. If I am convincing you this I am happy. It is one of the only things I know.

Love,
Marina

~

From: *yourmom93@hotmail.com*
Sent: *January-31-09 00:02:12 AM*
To: *marinagurtz@yahoo.com*

Marina,
Don't be mad at me.

I showed one of your e-mails to our parents. They were about to turn out the lights in their bedroom and

I worked up the nerve and went in and showed them. They read the beginning of it, maybe a line or two. Then he grabbed me. By the shoulders, really hard, and our father has not laid a finger on me in anger or affection since I hit puberty but I thought he was going to hit me, he starts roaring at me in Russian, then in English he goes why did you not show this before! He's shaking me and I'm sure he's going to pound me into the floor. But actually he starts crying, just bawling, and he pulls me tight to him and kisses me on the head. Our father had not kissed me since I turned thirteen. My mother's gripping him so hard her fingers leave red blotches in his arm. He howled, Marina. It was like he was losing you again.

That's not even the huge part. He's gone to the bank to cash in a bond or something. He's buying plane tickets for the three of us. We're coming to see you. I'm going to meet you! And you'll be getting e-mails from both of them soon, in Russian so you won't need to ask your pervert translator friend!

This is the most incredible thing that's ever happened to me. It was all true. They told me everything. They found your clothes by the river. They searched and searched for you. They were sure you were dead.

I'm sorry I didn't believe you, Marina. Thank you for writing to me. I can't wait to see you.

Love,
your sister,
Tasia.

~

From: **marinagurtz@yahoo.com**
Sent: **February-2-09 1:21:04 PM**
To: **yourmom93@hotmail.com**

Dear Tasia,

Thank you for this e-mail. I am very much with feeling because of it. Also I hope that our father has not got these airplane tickets.

Let me to explain this way I feel. I am not very much unhappy that you show my e-mail to our parents. I think this is okay. But I do not want them to come seeing me. I also do not want you to come seeing me. I know this may make hurt to you. I apologize already. This will be also my last e-mail to you for now.

I have lived here in Russia by alone since I was fifteen years. I have worked by alone, I have studied by alone, even as I have made this piece of family, with Mitya, I have done this by alone. This is not always making me happy, but it is making me with strength. Our mother and our father I am thinking may be very much good people, but what is truth is that they cared more for their selves and you than for me, because if they did not leave Russia so swift they would find me and I would be with them. And with you. And the life would be different.

I am happy if they know that I live, and you also. Let me say this thing about you, I have much feeling of love for you. I have loved writing with you. At some time in future it may be good to meet. But is not possible now. You must give time. Like Mitya gave time, and soon we will marry, you must give time. Someday we will write again, I am certain. My English will be wonderful! I will miss you very much. But I cannot continue like this. I ask forgiveness.

I realize I forget your birthday. Now you are sixteen, my sister. Happy birthday to you. I felt great love for you when you were a roundness in my mother's middle also. Yes, it is possible to love the thing you do not know.

Marina

~

From: **yourmom93@hotmail.com**
Sent: **February-3-09 02:33:14 AM**
To: **marinagurtz@yahoo.com**

You bitch. You selfish fucking bitch. How dare you. How DARE you. FUCK you. I hope you die and go to hell.

Your sister,
Tasia.

~

From: **yourmom93@hotmail.com**
Sent: **July-5-09 10:21:34 PM**
To: **marinagurtz@yahoo.com**

Marina, will you please write to me? Please. I'm sorry, okay? I'm trying to understand how you feel, but this is just cruel. Five months and *nothing* is just cruel. Maybe you aren't even at this e-mail address anymore. Where are you?

I'm a counsellor at an arts day camp this summer. I like it a lot. And I'm dating a guy who's a gentleman. Anyway. Not like you'd care.

I miss you.

Your sister,
Tasia.

~

From: **yourmom93@hotmail.com**
Sent: **October-16-09 2:14:57 PM**
To: **marinagurtz@yahoo.com**

http://leavesofspring.org/poetry-contest/first-place-Tasia
Kalnitsky-FirstLightSingsToTheGulag.html

Your sister,
Tasia.

~

From: **tasia.checks.emails@gmail.com**
Sent: **January-1-10 11:49:01 AM**
To: **marinagurtz@yahoo.com**

Marina,

Here's to a happy, healthy new year. I hope everything is good with you in Russia. My life is fine here. It's not long till I'm seventeen. They're already pressuring us in school to choose a career direction. My science marks are solid and our parents want me to go into medicine, but every day I find myself more drawn to literature and the arts. I'm reading constantly. Your (our) country really ain't such a slouch in that respect! Have you ever read Dostoevsky or Pushkin in the original? I look forward to talking to you about it someday.

Your sister,
Tasia.

∼

From: **marinagurtz@yahoo.com**
Sent: **April-26-10 08:27:14 AM**
To: **tasia.checks.emails@gmail.com**
CC: **yourmom93@yahoo.com**

My Tasia,
There is much to tell you, but today I tell only this.

Outside the house of Mitya and me there is a garden. It is small garden, but with enough room for what we plant. The earth is very hard, but somehow much grows. Both Mitya and I enjoy working at our garden. It is relaxing. There is simplicity. And last week something you wrote returned to me. I had wrote you that our father worked at mill where he made flowers, and you wrote and told that it is impossible to make flowers, that I had made mistake. But last week I stood with my husband in this garden, new green in hard black earth, and I thought of what you said and I was puzzled.

It is not impossible, Tasia. Of course it is not impossible.

Your sister,
Marina

A Much Loved Teacher

~

By the time Aaron approaches the accident, a couple of cars have already stopped, their bundled-up drivers crouched by the toppled motorcycle and the man sprawled on the icy asphalt beside it. The traffic means that Aaron has a clear look for maybe fifteen seconds. The motorcyclist, or one of those assisting him, has removed his helmet. His face is turned away from the road. He holds his chest as though something there is oozing out, or oozing within. It's only as Aaron is about to pass the scene that he catches sight of the victim's face and thinks he recognizes his old French teacher.

Mr. Shenkman. A good teacher, an extraordinary storyteller. For his seventh-grade students, Shenkman's stories took on mythic dimensions. He'd lived in Africa. He'd known Pierre Trudeau. At one point he'd known Trudeau in Africa. No less compelling were his stories set in their quiet suburban community — about his Jewish motorcyclists' club, or his eldest son's confrontations with teenaged anti-Semites. Between stories Mr. Shenkman reviewed vocabulary, verb conjugations. He was solidly built, not too tall, bald, with thick-rimmed glasses from behind which his eyes met yours with reserved intelligence and, if you earned it, great warmth. He was known to cultivate lasting relationships with certain students. Aaron was never one of them. Their relationship was respectful, unexceptional. He hasn't spoken to, or really thought about, Mr. Shenkman since he graduated from elementary school a decade ago. Until tonight.

He arrives home still preoccupied by what he saw. He paces his childhood bedroom, tries to decide what to do. Some of his seventh-grade friends were close with Shenkman, babysat their teacher's nieces and nephews; some of them might've been entrusted with his phone number. Maybe Lana Franklin, he thinks. In the seventh grade he hadn't known Lana very well, but they bumped into each other on campus a month ago and she suggested they grab coffee sometime, scribbled her number on a scrap of paper torn from her prettily engraved notebook.

She picks up right away. I didn't think I'd hear from you, she says. I've been meaning to call, he says. Happy you did. Listen, I think Mr. Shenkman's been in an accident, you remember him? There's a pause. Of course, she says. What kind of accident? I think he fell from his motorcycle. Fell. Yeah, there was ice all around. God. Yeah, I know. And you've spoken to him? No, that's the thing, I don't even know for sure that it was him, I couldn't see the guy's face clearly, but so I wanted to call him and make sure everything's okay and it occurred to me that you might have his number. I do, she says, and falls silent. He waits. Listens to her slow breathing on the line. I used to have the biggest crush on him, she says. Really, he says. Crazy, I know, he must've been over fifty even then. But there was something about him. Unknowable. No matter how much he told us about himself. Actually, the more he revealed, the less I felt I knew him. As if each story made the decoy Shenkman more lifelike while the real him made a run for it. She's silent again. He waits, rapt. Sorry, she says. Please, he says. Didn't mean to weird you out, she says, I promise I won't be like this if we go for coffee. I promise I won't spring bad news on you if we go for coffee. And if there's bad news? I'll lie, he says.

He dials Shenkman's number as soon as they hang up. He's concerned about the late hour, close to midnight—if his intuition proves false, he'll have alarmed the household for no reason. After five or six rings, a groggy female voice: Hello? Hi, says Aaron, very sorry to call so late, could I please speak to Leonard? It feels awkward, transgressive to use his teacher's first name. Who's calling, Mrs. Shenkman wants to know. He could just ask if her husband had been in an accident this evening. He doesn't. I used to be his student, he says. There's a hesitation. The sound of slow exertion: someone standing who'd rather not. Hang on, she says.

Hi, who's this? says Leonard Shenkman, and immediately Aaron's certain he's made a mistake, it was somebody else by the side of the ice-slicked road, he's called this man for no reason and now he has nothing to say.

Hi, this is Aaron Gold, you probably don't remember me, I — Sure I remember you, spacey kid, big hair, how're you doing? Fine, how are you? Retired now. So what's new, what's your life like these days? Good, listen, sorry to call so late, it's just — So you called, it's late, okay, now are you gonna catch me up or what?

Aaron hesitates. He's tempted to say goodbye, hang up as fast as possible; he's tempted to recite as a list all the accomplishments for which he's been recognized since grade school. He feels sure that anything he says will be listened to. I'm in university, he says. Good, do you like it? *Comme-ci comme-ca.* So leave. I'm almost finished. So stay. I plan to. What else? I've been painting. Oh yeah? Quite a lot actually, yeah. Ever consider going to school for it? Well, not really, not full-time anyway, but I'm enrolled in a program in Paris this spring and then I plan to travel around Europe a bit. Good too, be careful ... I plan to be in Europe myself this spring, Shenkman goes on. I need to take a little time. Been feeling a bit wrecked lately. Wrecked how? Silence. You probably would've understood better when you were twelve. A strange laugh, hard and abrupt. In the background, Shenkman's wife calls for him. I'll be a few minutes, says Shenkman. Turn out the lights, I can find my way in the dark.

Just a little wrecked, Aaron's old French teacher says. Probably this brutal weather. There were times like this when we were in Rhodesia. Zimbabwe. There it was the heat. You could just sit for days. Not do anything. Unhealthy. I remember a time when I went off into the

bush near our house with a rifle because we heard a rustling. Soon as I approached, the rustling stopped. So there
I was, gun in my hands, nothing to do with it. I could
hear the voices of the others back at the house. Didn't
feel like joining them again. So I just sat down where I
was. And then, maybe two yards away, this little family
of snakes crept out from beneath a cluster of plantains.
Five of them. Long. Black long things. The width of two
fingers. No clue what type of snake they were, didn't look
like any snake I'd ever seen before. They moved together. Towards the compound. Real slow, but that was their
direction. Towards my wife, and my sons, and all the locals we employed to help around the place. Those snakes
weren't interested in me at all. They moved right past me.
I could've walked away. But instead I got real close, pointed the gun, and put a bullet in each of them, fast. Black
goo. Explosions of shiny purple. Five bullets. Didn't both-
er me much to do it. Easy to rationalize in the moment.
My family was there. Or whatever. But what got me was
that even when I crouched over them and aimed, not one
of them looked my way. They didn't acknowledge me.
It was as if I wasn't there at all.

Soft breathing on the line. So I'll be in Europe for a
while this spring, Shenkman says, I'm going to Venice,
when are you in Paris? The end of May, Aaron says, his
voice faint. Let's meet up if you're in Italy while I'm
there, Shenkman says, I'll be by myself, my wife's not
coming, and Aaron says, okay.

They hang up. He sits on the edge of his bed. There's
nothing else he wants to do tonight, but even if there

were, he probably wouldn't be able to do it. He brushes his teeth, undresses, lies under the covers in his dark bedroom. He closes his eyes and tries to picture his old French teacher's face. Can't. Sees instead five sunbursts of blood on a jungle floor.

But thank God he wasn't in a motorcycle accident, he thinks. Thank God, thank God he wasn't in a motorcycle accident.

The Snake Crosses
the Tracks at Midnight

～

We drive south, park at the community centre, walk along the curb, as per the directions Lucy got from Shira Coffler in our Grade 12 Civics class. Traffic wings by us. I follow Lucy down a little path into the ditch, around the overpass. Gang tags mark the overpass's side: a dragon's head, teeth clamped around a bloodied serpent. We're headed into trees, the path in front of us dark.

"Did they bring lights?"

"They're making a fire."

We're in some sort of valley. Moonlight peeks through and I see a black stream to our right, hiccupping over rocks and twigs with belches of foam.

I grab Lucy's shoulders, squeeze a little. "Are you just trying to get me alone in the woods?"

She stops. She turns and looks at me. I'd meant something along the lines of: are you trying to murder me or steal my wallet? A little, unfunny joke. But she didn't hear it like that. We've had these moments before.

Lucy and I have known each other since we were four, when my house was two doors down from hers and our parents took advantage of our pre-pre-pubescent love affair — she was my girlfriend, and I liked to pinch her, apparently — for babysitting purposes. When my parents wanted to go to the movies on a Saturday night, they'd leave me with Lucy and the Friedmans; when Mr. and Mrs. Friedman wanted to spend time with their mistress or mistress, respectively, they'd deposit Lucy on our front stoop. We haven't discussed our early romance since puberty bodychecked us, but sometimes a ghost of it appears behind her eyes, and I think: it was real. What we felt then was real.

There's the sound of a train horn. Lucy looks up towards the sound, which is still distant, a rumour. Suddenly she's pushing me off the path, up a hill, where I trip, fall. Dry leaves crunch and I'm on my back. She's beside me. In a crouch. Close to me. I don't really want her, she's too known, but I have an erection. She doesn't touch me, doesn't even look at me. She stares at the tracks.

"What are we doing?" I ask.

"Waiting for the snake."

Maybe I should be more interested in her. I like girls. I like sex, the tastes I've had of it. I'm too particular. Or I'm too nervous. We're alone in the woods; this is how it could happen, if we both want it to. But she's not even looking at me.

"It's not coming. It must be going the other way."

She shakes her head. And she stands up and walks off as if nothing's happened.

I trail a few feet behind her. No questions; she'd give me no straight answers.

We spot a fire in ten minutes and arrive at a crowded, subdued party. Our classmates sit on logs, on the ground. There are dry leaves and twigs nearby and I worry the fire might spread, create a secret inferno that we must secretly squelch. Souvenirs of alcohol are littered around: cans and bottles, small puddles from spills. Shira Coffler and Michael Stein spot us; Stein tells us to make ourselves at home. We find an empty spot in the circle and plunk ourselves down. I don't know most of the people here. Lucy doesn't seem to, either. There's the beanpole self-professed "player" from my math class, his arm around a petite blonde; the three Gothy Russian girls never seen apart, dubbed the Dark Sisters of the Revolution by certain wits; and Brian Waters, who plays water polo but is sometimes snubbed by other jocks because of his freely confessed affection for Broadway musicals. Waters offers us a joint. "Toke?"

"Noke," I say, which makes him think I'm already high, which is incorrect, or that I'm a complete fucking knob, which is correct. Lucy takes a few long drags.

"How long have people been here?" I ask Waters.

He leans back, rests on his elbows. "Not long. Since eleven maybe."

That's all I can think of to say to him. Not that he minds: he's lost to us, embroiled in a love affair with the night sky and his navel. For a very long time, I do nothing but sit still and wear a tense half-smile and eavesdrop on gossip. Crickets play cricket in the bushes. Lucy

talks about *Evita* with Waters. I chew on my lip. I've got a
few basic points in common with the others here: immin-
ent end of high school, inability to imagine a future, constant low-level terror/longing re: sex. So it's weird that I
have no desire to say anything to any of them besides
Lucy. Finally, worried I'll fall asleep if I stay silent, I turn
to a short, ripped guy in a Nirvana T-shirt and say, apropos of the insects on my jeans: "I'm so glad there are more
spiders than mosquitoes here, you know?"

He looks at me with his mouth open a sliver. "Wha?"

I shake my jeans. "Spiders. They eat mosquitos. So it's
okay if I've got the former on my pants, because it means
I won't get bitten by the latter. You know?"

He looks at me with terrible intensity. "You're so high,
man."

The bellow of the train rises. Lucy shoots to her feet,
wheels towards the sound. "Come on, we're going to miss
it!" she shout-whispers at me. She grabs me by the arm
and marches me across the clearing, up a hill. A few heads
by the fire turn to watch us.

"What are you doing!"

"Come on! You've gotta run!"

When we're halfway up the hill, she stops. We turn
and I can see the train tracks, the graffiti'd overpass, and,
approaching quickly, the lights of the Canadian National. Lucy tugs at my arm. "Look. Look. Watch this."

The train starts across the overpass. Lucy giggles
like a little girl.

And I see what she wants me to see. The fence at the
side of the overpass allows light from the train to pass

through in fragments. A pattern is created. The light from the train cuts up, down, over, up, down, over, like a light show, a performance held just for us, free of charge. The train is a snake, slithering across the tracks. Lucy's arm coils around mine. The light from the train barrels on, and on, and on: up, down, over, and again. A snake in the night.

"See? I told you it was worth it. We could've seen it even better from the path."

The train barrels east; its light leaves with it.

Moon remains. I can see Lucy's eyes. Green.

"Cool," I say, just barely.

~

When Lucy and I were seven, our families went on a picnic together, and it was a scary experience for our parents because they thought Lucy and I had gotten lost. For two hours they scrambled around the park in search of us, my mother crying, Lucy's father shouting at strangers, demanding to know if anyone had seen a skinny little boy with a pigtailed little girl. When finally they found us, they yelled at us for twenty minutes. Her father shook me; my mother wagged a finger in Lucy's tiny, uncomprehending face. We were packed into minivans, driven home, and sent to our rooms with the sternest reprimands.

But we hadn't meant to cause trouble. Lucy and I had felt abandoned. We'd been walking in circles around a huge elm tree, discussing why we can buy animals from stores but they can't buy us, when suddenly we noticed that all the adults, plus my sister, plus Lucy's brothers, had disappeared. We stood still, silent, stony-faced. Looked out over the empty field. They had left us all alone. So we decided, in that clearheaded way I lost with the first breath of adolescence, that we should just stay put and wait for our prodigal guardians to return. I escorted a ladybug off Lucy's arm. We lay in the grass, under the sun and the sky which had clouds but not too many clouds, and we chatted. I said what do you think we'll be when we grow up and she said astronauts. I agreed with her. She said what do you think that cloud is and I said an elephant. She agreed with me. I said that cloud is a train and she said no it's a box of cereal on its side. We proceeded across the sky: a noodle, a cheetah, a bird (which actually was a bird). She asked me where I wanted to live when I was older, and I said I don't think you can choose, I think when you turn eighteen the wind starts to blow really hard and by that point you have a special flying suit, so when the wind blows with all that fury it lifts you up, off the ground, throwing you around the world over majestic peaks and valleys, until finally, when your flying suit is wearing out, the wind sets you down in the place you're supposed to be, with the people you're supposed to be with, and you're okay. You're okay. You're just okay, I said. And she held me through the afternoon until our parents found us.

~

At around one in the morning Brian Waters keels over. Efforts to revive him fail. Alcohol poisoning, somebody says, and I realize I don't know whether that means he's going to die or he's just out for the night. Panic ripples. One of the Goth girls pulls out her phone and calls an ambulance. She doesn't know how to describe where we are, though, plus she probably doesn't want to, so she tells the paramedics to meet us by the overpass. I join an overmanned effort to carry Waters through the unmarked woods — to go back along the path would take too long — and we set out, bearing our wounded, Lucy so close behind me I can feel her breath on the back of my neck. We emerge into the light of the street and climb out of the ditch, lower Waters to the damp grass by the side of the road, in the glare of passing traffic. The ambulance arrives. The paramedics lift Waters onto a gurney, load him into the vehicle. Michael Stein goes with them, his face sombre. Responsibility: it sits in the gut, sticks. The wind's picked up.

Lucy's arms are crossed, hands folded beneath them to keep warm.

"How'd you know about the lights from the train?" I ask.

I regret the words the moment they're out of my mouth.

"Sometimes I've gone down there to read." She doesn't meet my eye. "Sometimes I've stayed into the evening."

She looks so old to me. She looks thirty, a hundred years old, like she's seen everything, outlived every mystery, and I want to go back, to ask her again and hear her answer: What lights? What train? There is no train. There has never been a train. What you saw, old man, was a snake.

An Old Friend

~

So I'm at this bar, busy place on the Esplanade the guys from my firm visit after work. I don't often join them, my home life appeals to me and I see my family little enough as it is, but this time I've gone down for a quick drink, I think this is a Monday evening, long week ahead. I'm sitting at a table with Aaron Gold and Joe Harris, both of them guys around my age, we have work in common and similar taste in movies and music, we get along. There's a certain testosterone quotient at the table, definitely, but none of us are the loud type, neither Aaron nor Joe nor I ever went in for the cutthroat stuff, we came to the law as idealistic, let's say quasi-socialistic young guys, we were smart and we were interested in things like human rights law, social justice, advocacy for the voiceless and so on, and we never abandoned the spirit of that, but, it happens, we all got married, two out of three of us had kids, and our politics changed as we spent more time in the world. Now we make more money than we ever dreamed of making, way more than our fathers ever made, and sometimes the work's interesting, it's always demanding, which is fine, keeps you sharp, but it's good to grab a drink and ease the pressure.

So I'm sitting there having a beer, laughing with my friends about our belligerent boss, when I notice that Joe and Aaron are staring past me. I stop talking, I look where they're looking and I see this guy, around my age, standing by our table. He's been waiting for a chance to cut in. He's tall, pretty thin, brown guy with dark hair trimmed close, could be Pakistani, Lebanese. Dressed neatly, crisp white shirt and black slacks, loud red cufflinks. Don't think I've ever seen him before.

"You don't remember me," he says.

And I'm like, "Sorry, we know each other?"

"Can I buy you a drink?"

"Good of you, but why would you do that?"

"For old times' sake."

So now I'm thoroughly confused. I can tell that Joe and Aaron have their guard up. There's something pro-vocative in the guy's tone — half ingratiating, half iron-ic. I don't understand it, don't like it. "Do we know each other," I say to him again.

"Yorkhill."

And then I know who he is.

My heart starts to hammer, I'm cold and I'm hot and I don't want my friends to see something's fucked, so I get up and go, "I'll be back in a sec," with as much of a wry glance as I can muster.

I walk ahead of him to the bar. We sidle in among

the schmoozers, he asks me what I'm drinking and I reply mechanically, I'm so distracted, shaken by him. I'm like, "What are you doing here?"

"I work nearby."

"Yeah? Doing what?"

"Insurance," says Mohammed. And he pays for our scotch.

Mohammed Khan. Terror of the sixth grade. I wasn't a tough kid, I was openhearted and trusting, he was the product (I knew even then) of a family life fraught with emotional violence and other violence, and he paid that violence forward to me. He forbade the others in our class to be friends with me, and they obeyed him, such was his power. He belittled me, he insulted me without provocation and without end, after a while he had me convinced of his superiority, and whatever sense of self I had at twelve began to crumble. I was a case study in preteen anxiety and depression, and I think he knew it, revelled in it. I dreaded going to school, my parents sent me to a shrink, didn't help, nothing helped till I switched schools and never saw him again, till today.

But look at me now, I think, I'm not that frightened little boy anymore, I'm a grown-up, I'm married, I have a child of my own, I make a good living and dress well and laugh deeply, there's no way in which I'm vulnerable to Mohammed Khan anymore, so get a grip, I say to myself.

"I know you work at Gowlings," he goes. "Mitchell Klein told me. I've followed your career."

"Oh yeah? And you're in insurance."

"Sun Life. Risk management."

"I thought you were going to be an actor."

He flashes that thin, ironic smile.

"I hear you're married," he says.

"Mitchell Klein tell you that too?"

"Yes, actually."

"I haven't seen him in years."

"He's an architect. His company did the new condo developments near Fort York."

"Pillars of society, our class."

"Cheers."

We drink.

"You married?" I ask him.

"No."

"Girlfriend?"

"No."

"You were the only one in our class who had a girlfriend."

"Was I?"

"Diane," I say. "You flaunted it like crazy. You'd go everywhere together, holding her hand."

"I remember very little about that time."

There's a pause. We drink, watch the flow of others mingling, flirting.

"I was very unhappy," he says. "I didn't believe there would ever be a future. I was sure I would die before I turned into my parents, whatever, I'd kill myself. I thought grade six, grade seven, maybe grade eight, that would be the rest of my life, and I'd better make the most of it. I wanted to unleash my shitstorm on the world, I wanted to give the world a beating. I was not a normal boy."

"Oh yeah?" Sadistic, vain, a cruel wit. That's what I remember. "I think you were perfectly normal."

"I'm not saying I …"

I down the rest of my scotch. "Thanks for the drink, man." And I turn to go back to my friends. He puts his hand on my arm. I stare at it. He removes it. "Did you not hear what I said? Thank you for the drink, have a nice life—"

"My first wet dreams were about you."

He hasn't said it quietly, but nobody around us is paying attention.

"I hated you. I was twelve years old and I was convinced I was a monster, I knew my parents would kill me if they so much as suspected … they would kill me, no figure of speech, my father would take me by the neck and strangle me till I was dead."

His hands are shaking.

I watch him. I watch him drink. I notice for the first time how narrow his shoulders are, how frail he is, all jagged edges, nerve and bone. I think of him at twelve, alone in his parents' house, terrified, crying himself to sleep at the thought that there might be something horribly wrong with him. I pity him. I do.

And then I think of my daughter. I think of my beautiful daughter. Starting school in the fall.

And what I do then is I gather a wad of phlegm, I clear it from the very back of my throat, and I spit my great wad of phlegm in Mohammed Khan's face. Plastered across his face, along with my spit, is a look of astonishment and—I'm sure I see it—childlike fear. Before he can say anything, I'm walking away. I call back over my shoulder: "Likely story."

Aaron and Joe are waiting for me, eager to hear. They've seen none of it.

Joe's like, "Who was that?"

"An old friend."

Fifteen minutes later I'm still shaking all over.

All That Flies from You

~

Last time I watched from in front of Diesel Jeans, the shop closest to the action. Young, both of them. Him: twenty at most. Her: a mature eighteen. They took a long time. Big floor-to-ceiling window behind them; three planes took off on the nearest runway in the time they took. I could hear a bit. Her: promise me you'll e-mail, soon as you get there. Him: I'll never forget you. A close dynamic. As though almost equals in affection. If possible.

They're in front of security. His arm is comfortable around her hips, she squeezes his waist, there's something of habit there, you get the sense that even if this was a fling it's one that's had a bit of longevity. My guess: both boy and girl American. Or Canadian. She speaks too softly for me to pin down an accent. Possible scenarios for meeting: they could've been on one of the subsidized tours for young diasporic Jews (but too short-term for the intimacy on display); working with Sar-El, the military volunteer service (but too much that's tentative, almost fragile in his manner); volunteers on a kibbutz. That last one seems to me most likely. It's how I met my first girlfriend, as a Canadian volunteer on Kibbutz Dan. A hundred years ago.

She touches his face. He kisses her, gently. This is a pattern I've observed before. First the couple will share a small, chaste kiss, as if parting is a delicate matter. One or both will then recognize the absurdity, the vanity of such restraint and kiss the other with passion. So it happens here. He, the flyer, heads into security without a backwards glance. She, the remaining, waits and watches for a few minutes as he passes through the metal detector. Then a few minutes more. Eventually she moves from the gate. She sits at a table and stares at her hands. If you watch closely, if you're a man like me who has trained himself to watch closely, you can see her shoulders tremble.

I'm tapped on the shoulder. The Diesel Jeans clerk, tall Sephardi girl, frowns. *Ata rotzey mashehu?* What is it I want. I want a one-way ticket to Hawaii. I want two decades returned to me in mint condition. I want my dog to be loyal to me and quit running away. *B'seder*, I say, and leave the store, leave the terminal, go find my car in the lot.

Each week this is my Sunday afternoon.

~

A Sunday late in May. I'm seated outside the airport McDonald's. I've ordered a coffee. You've got to order something; otherwise they harass you. I recognize this is the same the world over, but in Tel Aviv when you talk harassment you're talking almost bodily.

Already today I've seen an extraordinary goodbye. Identical twin brothers, embracing, crying, one says: When will I see you again? The other touches his brother's cheek, says: When will I see you again? They were closer than lovers. Nothing in sight interested each man more than the other's face, all but indistinguishable from his own.

A few more swing by in quick succession. A mother and daughter: mom bristling with protective nerves, girl straining to break loose. An elderly couple: reserved, aware of people watching, how public a place this is for demonstration. A whole extended Asian family, probably Thai, sending off their university-aged son, who walks through the gates with shy pride. I sip my coffee. There's a lull in traffic at security, a lull in goodbyes. My thoughts drift to ancient history.

Around noon, two girls arrive, only one of them carrying luggage. My reveries break. They're young girls, eighteen or nineteen. They stand and talk, their backs to me. Can't hear a word, though I can tell their rapport is easy, low-key. They kiss each other on the cheek and part. The remaining girl lingers at the gate. As soon as she turns a fraction of an inch, I know without a doubt she is my daughter.

She sits at a table, pulls out a cell phone. My daughter Hailey. My daughter who lives now with her mother in New York. Who I had no idea was in Israel. Whom I have not seen for two years, five months, and fourteen days. And who, though so close, does not see me. The phone is to her ear, but she's not talking. Checking messages. My daughter to whom I haven't spoken in six months. She used to call me when she got lonely. Now there's a boyfriend. My daughter who didn't speak to me for a year after she and Liza left. Who, when finally she called, told me I should get a dog. For company. Which I did.

As soon as she puts down the phone, before she has a chance to leave, I approach her. I'm not a coward. I tap her on the shoulder, say: Hi stranger. She turns and sees me, takes me in. An unsure smile. Oh wow, she says, hi. I didn't know you were here, I say, you didn't call. I've been busy, she says, sorry. I ask how long she's been in Israel. Since the beginning of the month, she tells me. An organized tour. She stayed an extra two weeks, flies home today. She looks healthy, has gotten some colour. When's your flight? I ask. Later this afternoon, she says. I ask her what she was planning on doing till then. I dunno, she says, sit around I guess, read. I tell her I'll buy her lunch. There's an awful moment when I'm not sure if she's going to agree. But she nods. Cautious. As though considering what harm there might be.

We have shwarma together in a corner of the waiting lounge. I thought she was a vegetarian. She says she stopped. Why should we be kinder to the cows than to the plants? We talk about how she's enjoying school. Brown University, philosophy major, art history minor. We talk about her boyfriend, Robert, a nice guy, pre-med, two years older. Discuss her mother, who's unhappy, not interested in changing. As before. As ever. We don't say a word about her brother, my son, whose death on duty in Nablus precipitated their move back to America. There would be little point. Why spoil a nice lunch? Why pretend as though a chance meeting on a Sunday afternoon in May might change anything? The grounded way she looks at me gives me great pleasure. She doesn't feign closeness, but neither does she lash out. When she asks me if there's a woman in my life these days, she does so with an adult equanimity that bowls me over. I'm proud of her. I don't know her at all. I couldn't be prouder of her. Her question I deflect. It's nice that you met this Robert, I say. When I ask her what it's been like to return to Israel after so long, and not as a child now, she tells me she thinks it's a beautiful country, really fascinating, though she doesn't think she'll ever live here again, she's not religious, religion makes her uncomfortable, she doesn't really believe. Me neither, I say. I know, she says. I remember.

We've talked for almost two hours. She has to make her way to her departure gate. I walk her from the restaurant to where I first noticed her, by security. She looks at me. As if to say: Here we are, this is it, now we say goodbye. My daughter will go back to the States, to her studies and her boyfriend. I'll go back to my apartment, to my dog. I won't get a kiss on the cheek. Anyone watching would think us acquaintances at best. Maybe distant relatives. Bye, says my daughter. I don't walk away. I don't smile and send her off. I am incapable of it. I am incapable of parting. Hailey, I say. Just her name. Don't make it complicated, Dad, she says. But I'm not trying to. I'm not trying to at all. And anyone watching would know it. Anyone watching would recognize at once this rarest of sightings: the animal failing itself. The man, placed in a situation most primal, like sex, like holding his new-born child, not having the faintest idea how it's done.

The Baker's Apprentice

~

The boy wanted to be a baker. He loved baked goods and the idea of creating simple, essential things. On a whim, he left a résumé at his favourite bakery, an old family business downtown. To his surprise, he received a call. Could he come for an interview, maybe Thursday?

He arrived punctually for his appointment. The baker, an elderly Jewish man, short and bespectacled, led him through the store: through the back, by the oven, the tables for kneading, bags of yeast; and through the front, where racks overflowed with bagels, *challahs*. How long have you been here? asked the boy. Since the forties, said the baker. My father, he started this bakery when he came over. He built it up, he had no help, he was a real *mensch*. I worked here when I was about your age — how old are you, eh? Sixteen, said the boy, but he said it like *Twenty*. Sixteen, said the baker, I worked here when I was sixteen, summers, wished I was doing something else, there were girls around, we lived nearby — sixteen, I remember that. My own kids, they worked here when they were in high school too. You're in high school? How're your marks, you a good student? The boy nodded. The old baker looked at him, sized him up, less like a judge than like a tailor, and said: Come tomorrow morning, 4:30. We'll make *challahs* for Shabbat.

The boy stared at his hands on the subway ride home, imagined them kneading moist, puffy cords of dough. His fingers were long, a bit knobby at the tips. *Challahs*, thought the boy, a mythical bread, loaves pregnant with occasion. His mother picked him up at the subway station and wanted to know how the interview had gone. Fine, he said. I'm going to make *challahs*. Really, said his mother. She laughed gently, as though tousling his hair, which he wouldn't let her do. Do you know how? she asked. He gazed out the window, at the endless succession of tidy suburban houses. I'll learn, he said.

The boy arrived at the bakery the next morning as the pale dawn broke. The baker demonstrated — how to mix eggs, flour, yeast, how to knead the dough into strips, how to weave, layer, smooth — the boy imitated in turn. Hands pressed down on hands. *Nu*, okay, like this, said the baker. They loaded tray after tray into the oven. Later they wiped down the soiled countertop, brushed away crumbs, and the boy thought: there's nothing profound in this, I can't imagine anything simpler — and to think I built it up so much. After the oven was loaded, the baker invited the boy out to the back porch for a smoke. The boy didn't smoke, didn't much want to, but was prepared to accept if the baker offered. The baker didn't offer. It's nice, said the baker, to see somebody take an interest. Most of the young people I meet today aren't interested in anything. Wouldn't get off their asses if people weren't pushing and shoving. I have kids your age, a little older, twins, she's at the university, he's trying to start a business with his friends, he's on the Internet, twenty-two this kid, he wants to start his own business? Used to be a guy would bust his *tuchus* a little first, pay his dues. The boy nodded. And at the appointed hour they went into the bakery, pulled up the blinds, and unlocked the door, ready for the day's first customers.

The boy rose at 3:30 AM on Mondays, Wednesdays, and Fridays, baked the morning's goods with the baker, helped to open the shop, and ran to catch the streetcar, the subway north, the bus towards his high school. He came to class haggard; his teachers and classmates thought him disinterested, aloof; he cultivated the impression and didn't properly button his shirt. They think my nights are wild, he imagined. They think I'm with an older woman. They think I mix with crooks and drug dealers, I'm part of the underworld, they'll get the police to raid my locker. As he sat, exhausted, in his English class, he felt a certain satisfaction at how he was different, how the eyes that searched him on his entrance saw only what he chose to show them. His idea of himself on those days buoyed him till classes' end.

It was only later, as he walked home, shut the front door of his parents' house, settled at the computer with a cup of microwaved noodle soup, that he'd be overwhelmed by a sudden melancholy. He'd imagine the older woman he didn't know and didn't sleep with, the dangerous, thrilling life he didn't lead, and, as he nursed his soup for lack of anything to do once he'd finished it, would say to himself: I'm passionate about nothing, I act on little whims like this baking thing, but nothing drives me besides curiosity ... so what happens when my curiosity has been satisfied in every way? Can you reach that point? Do people roll over and die when they reach that point?

At dawn the next day he asked the baker, who was not young: Does curiosity dry up? His rolling pin in motion, hands twisting, relaxing, twisting, the baker replied: it turns into disbelief. I was curious about the world too, I wanted to travel, I wanted to sleep with women, I was restless. Now it's not curiosity, now I've been with women and I can't believe they exist, I'm filled with amazement — I love women, I've been married to three of them, still I'm in disbelief. I can't believe my children are able to have businesses on a computer screen and make more money than I do. It's hard enough to believe I've got kids at all. I probably wouldn't believe it at all if I didn't come in here every morning. I have kids, therefore I work; I work, therefore I have kids. Funny logic, but that's how it goes. So what, thought the boy, does this work mean for me? Instead he said: And that you're a baker, are you in disbelief about that too? The baker placed a finished loaf into a row, completing the tray. No, said the baker. That's a curiosity.

The boy was invited to the baker's house for dinner. The baker told the boy his parents were welcome too, but the boy not-so-accidentally forgot to pass the invitation along. His parents were decent enough people, but in their striving to be affectionate they would betray some confidence, hold him up, if not to scorn, then to light-hearted condescension, which was worse. In his suit, the boy surfaced from the subway. The night was cool. The streetcar clanged past, forlorn faces peering out from the soft yellow light within, light that seemed to the boy, that evening, ancient and on the verge of going out forever. I'm on my way to dine with the baker, the boy thought, pleased and excited. He wondered who else would be there. Certainly the baker's wife, but which of the baker's children? Would they resent him, look at him as the usurper of their inheritance? Would they remind him of himself, those apprentices to the baker far longer moulded than he? As he approached the baker's house, he untied his tie and buried it in his jacket pocket. He didn't want to show up the baker's sons.

He arrived nervous to the point of exhaustion, but the baker's wife put him immediately at ease. She hugged him, smiled at him, her face warm, eyes sly, asked him: You didn't get lost? It's cold outside. He shook his head; he breathed in the smells of the baker's house. The baker lived in a house full of spices and salts. You look very nice, said the baker's wife, it was sweet of you to get dressed up, he's told me all about you. And she looked at the boy with something resembling pride. He's not home yet, she said, you can wait in the living room with the kids, they'll be happy to entertain you. Are all your kids eating with us? asked the boy, as the gentle plink of a piano sounded in the next room. The two youngest, the twins, they're the only ones who still live at home, thank goodness.

She led him around the corner—and there, in a worn armchair, was the baker's son; at the upright piano, the baker's daughter. They were older than him, but not by much. He could see only the side of the daughter's face. She played a simple *étude* in a major key. Her black shirt clung snugly to her shoulders, her arms. White hands crept out; long white fingers. Though her crescendos were subdued, the boy could see her chest swell with them. She was no bigger than him; older, but no bigger. He longed to touch her—the dancing fingers, the languid, tender arms. Yet there was nothing coarse about his feeling for her. She could never be anonymous for him, never *girl*, never *woman*. She was the baker's daughter, the daughter of the baker, the master of his craft. The *étude* sunk low, grew reflective; her chest rose. Perhaps the baker's wife had been a pianist; perhaps for years the house had been full of apprenticeship, the man and boys kneading, weaving, the girls and woman swelling the house with song, straining towards a mastery that would arrive coupled with the obligation of transmission, filling the house with apprenticeship again, through the generations. I'll just be in the kitchen, said the baker's wife. The boy and the baker's son, tall and gaunt, made introductions. My father tells me you'll make a fine baker, said the baker's son. He's told me he's real proud of your business, said the boy, wondering if the baker's son were lying too. The baker's daughter turned her head at the sound of his voice, gave him a thin smile. It danced up his spine.

At dinner the boy sat beside the baker, who smiled at his wife and said: This one will make a fine addition to the profession. The baker's son laughed, said: Ever consider that he might not want to make bagels all his life? The boy didn't mind the tension. He was preoccupied. The baker's daughter captured all his attention. He was drawn to the fiddlings of her long, white fingers with the cutlery. At first he stole glances, afraid to be caught, to offend her or his hosts. But soon he began to stare. What if they got married? He too would be the baker's son ...

There was a knock at the front door. The boy, startled, watched as the baker's daughter excused herself from the table. She returned with her black-clad arm and white hand around the waist of a man: a thick man with thick-rimmed glasses, in his twenties. The man's hand — large, rough — toyed with the fabric of her sleeve. She slipped her fingers into his. Her hand was swallowed, crushed, yet she seemed not to mind. The thick man exchanged greetings with the baker. I'm going to stay over at his place tonight, said the baker's daughter. She kissed the baker and went out with the other.

The room was now colder, its lights harsher. The boy stared at his plate. Here again was the despair that visited him at idle moments — the certainty, the absolute, unshakeable certainty that nothing mattered, nothing could matter, nothing he was or did would ever matter. Yet this despair made no sense. True, the baker's daughter wouldn't marry him; too small, too polite and sweet-tempered, too much of a dreamer, he was clearly not the type of boy that bakers' daughters spent time with. But the baker still glanced at him fondly. He still had dessert to look forward to. The next day at school, he would still walk into class and feel distinguished by an air of irresistible mystery. He would still be the baker's apprentice.

Yet for the rest of the evening he could think of nothing to say.

The next day was Friday. Today they would make *challahs* for Shabbat. In the doorway at dawn, the baker studied the boy for a moment longer than usual. You look unwell, said the baker. I'm tired, said the boy. It's really early.

They made bread together. The baker led, the boy followed. But this morning the boy felt impatient, didn't want to be anyone's apprentice any longer, and he tried to weave tighter, more perfect loaves than the baker's. Do I not bake just as many bagels and rolls? thought the boy. He should be the baker just because he's older? They readied the trays to load them into the oven. But as he glanced at the loaves, the baker hesitated. He read the shape of the unbaked bread with his hands, twisted the tray to inspect the other side. He looked at the boy, mystified and disturbed. These are all wrong, said the baker, the old baker without an heir. Can you explain this? The boy shrugged.

The boy quit his job later that day, his resignation tendered in a phone message left after business hours. In the message he gave his mailing address so he could be sent the remainder of the money he was owed. His marks improved again. Without the pre-dawn commute, he was alert again in school. He lost his absentee mystique, though he had to admit that it may have existed in no one's eyes but his own. His parents thought his decision sensible, responsible. There would be plenty of time to work, after all.

A little more than a year later, the boy, who'd gotten his driver's license, sat in the back seat of his father's car with his lips pressed into a classmate's navel. It was his first such encounter. He felt tired, strangely, insistently tired, but grateful, too, and he drew the girl towards him. He sucked her bottom lip, teased her teeth with his tongue, as if he knew how it were done. He slid his hand beneath her shirt and she nodded, didn't push it away. He pushed and pressed; he kneaded, he shaped. He lost track of which hands were hers and which his. But now she was squeezing his wrist. What, he said. You kiss too hard, she said. He let go of her. He felt far away from her, from everybody. Yet what did it matter? The girl, kissing, expectations, disappointment. He could hardly remember her name. A world full of people making needful things, making sense — when had he believed in that? His face grew hot with shame.

He told her he was sorry, helped her fix her shirt. They were silent, embarrassed, while he drove her home. When she had gone, he sat in the parked car for a long time, watching porch lights flicker into life, his thin and knobby hands wrapped tight around the wheel as the sky grew dark.

Rhapsody

~

Thomas and I are seated at the bar, close to the piano. We'd been wandering around the West Village, our freshman faces getting us turned away from a string of venues, when I spotted the lovely singer of show tunes through the window. Let's try here, I suggested, and Thomas was an easy sell. He usually is. A lad of outstanding piety, he's less concerned than I am about sex and so is more relaxed. He sleeps with guilt on a regular basis; guilt is tender and attentive.

Tall, curvy, in her twenties, with wavy red hair, the chanteuse turns to the two of us after her song and says: "You guys smile a lot."

There's an older man a few seats down from us at the bar, and he takes this opportunity, our moment in the limelight, to catch my eye. "Can I buy you boys drinks?" I flop around for a moment like a seal losing his fish. He senses my concern. "No strings attached," he adds. My friend, emboldened by confidence in his own chastity,

says: "Sure!" I feel this is a sticky move. I go along with
it.

Our solicitor is about sixty, short and wiry and well
groomed; a hint of boyishness abides beneath his wrinkles. He is, can be nothing other than, a regular in this
bar. He wears the room with ease. He doesn't appear
drunk, though many in the 30-plus crowd seem to know
how to hide it.

Some verbal scuffling with the bartender confirms
that 21 is, non-negotiably, the legal drinking age in the
United States. We go with Cokes. We talk to Saul, who's
introduced himself with a firm handshake. I can learn
something about flirtation from Saul. His manner is coat-
ed in harmlessness but taut with intent. It's sexy, or it
would be, were I at all interested. He asks us where we're
from. Toronto, I say. How did we meet each other? Oh, we
went to high school together. We didn't meet over the
Internet or something?

Oh.

It's clear that Saul is attracted to men. The pianist,
who is a man, is flirting with the bartender, who is a man.
The group of four middle-aged women in a nearby booth
appear to be, possibly in various combinations, more than
friends. Apparently we're in a gay bar.

Now Saul says something silly. "You ever want to be
in a porno film?" I blink several times; Thomas furrows
his brow, perplexed. Saul tells us he thinks we're beautiful
boys. Thomas finally gets it. I worry he's about to blanch
and whip out his Aramaic and do sixty Hail Marys, but
I have no need to worry. My pal is a smooth operator. He

tells Saul he thinks I'm more beautiful, I tell Saul I think Thomas is more beautiful, and so a heated argument begins. Saul arbitrates and ends it by saying that Thomas has the hair and I the face, "the sweet *faccia*." Insecurity insists I read his judgment as a lie. Still, I thank him.

A draught from the opened door makes me shiver. I'm starting to feel guilty for not correcting Saul's assumptions. But the lovely singer's set is coming to an end and Saul's advances have given me a shot of confidence. She sings a pristine top note; the drunk lesbians in the booth hoot; Saul leans over to talk politics with Thomas. As the object of my Saturday night affections walks from the piano to where she's deposited her winter accessories at the back of the bar, I trail behind her. My hands tremble. She's slipped into her sleeves by the time I heave my heart into my throat.

"So that was great," I say. "Like really great. What a great set."

She turns and takes me in with a charmed curiosity, as if I'm a talking cocker spaniel. "Well, thank you."

"So how do you get started with this stuff? I mean, you're a singer. That's wicked. So do you, like, what, make a demo tape and then send it around? That sort of thing?"

"Yeah, that sort of thing. Are you an aspiring musician?"

"Well, sorta. I mean no. But I can play the guitar. Sorta."

She gives me a bemused look.

"Look at how straight you are," she says.

Um.

"Right? You're not gay?"

"Well, no. I mean not in the traditional sense. Like I'm not going to go home with our new friend at the bar there. Even though I'm sure he's a nice guy. But, like, I dunno. I could love a guy. Sure. Love is love."

"That's a very delicate answer ..."

"Steven."

"You're what, nineteen?"

"Sure."

"Have you ever been with another boy?"

"Okay, no. But that's more a matter of chance, isn't it? Like if you find someone compatible who happens to be the same gender—"

"But you'd probably rather sleep with me. For instance."

"No, I, yeah, but that's not the—"

"Steven."

Her eyes are very blue.

"Okay. Yes. I'd rather sleep with you." I take quite a deep breath. "So ... is that a possibility?"

She seems to give it due consideration.

"I don't think so. Sorry."

The confidence with which Saul fuelled me forms a puddle on the floor. "Oh. Why not?"

"Because you're crazy young. For starters."

"I'm not that young. How the hell old are you, anyway?"

"Take care, Steven."

She blows me a kiss and makes her way to the exit.

Blood rushes to my face. I think of a thousand things I should've said.

Thomas is laughing with Saul. I clap a hand on my friend's shoulder and he glances up, sees my expression, loses his smile. "No luck?"

"I mean…"

"Ah."

Saul gives me a sympathetic look. "Your pal tells me you're straight."

"Oh yeah? What did he tell you about himself?"

"Things I would never, ever repeat in respectable company." He pats Thomas on the thigh. They both smile.

I'm beginning to feel nauseous. The ladies in the booth are singing *Yellow Submarine*. Thomas is confusing me. I'm sweating. I really want to take off my clothes. I really want to take off my clothes with someone else. But I don't like older men that way. "I'm getting tired."

Thomas frowns. "Oh. So you wanna go?"

"Can we?"

"I guess so. Yeah."

I can see that this has depressed Saul. I don't feel great about that, but my claustrophobia is mounting. The piano man seemed talented, but now it's as if he's playing *Heart and Soul* over and over again.

I grab my jacket. I toss money (those pale bills the colour of melancholy) at the bartender. He slides it back across the bar and tells me Saul has picked up our tab. Thank you, Saul. Thomas follows close behind me and, with plenty of eyes on our exit, we're back in the crisp chill of the West Village in December, remnants of the year's last leaves crunching beneath our feet.

We don't look at each other as we walk. When we arrive at Christopher Park, we sit on a bench. The park is poorly lit. I can hardly see Thomas. Down the street, a pack of college guys clown around with the one female friend in their midst, take turns doing the tango with her, ignore that she seems obviously to be annoyed. It turns my stomach. I consider the possibility that I might hate sex. Or at least all the dirt that clings to it. It's midnight.

"How you doing?" I say to Thomas.

"Mm. Good." He seems distracted.

"Are you?"

"What?"

"Gay."

"No."

I think for a second. "You wanna kiss each other or something?"

He looks at me without judgment. "Not really."

"Me neither. Not particularly."

As we walk home, steam funnels up from underground and cloaks the street. For a moment, passing through it, I feel like I could disappear.

Faithful

~

I.

He's at a cocktail party. On the rooftop, in the moonlight. He's talking to Phil Goldman: loud, and a loud tie. Talking about golf, or Phil is; then fishing. Masculine bonding rituals, boring to him. He made an effort, upon leaving the academy and entering the productive economy so-called, to acquaint himself with such things, to learn how to look at ease on the links, hooking bait. But this was narcolepsy-inducing, and he's always found, probably it's a liability, that once he tires of something he can't bring himself to drudge through for very long. We've bought a boat, Phil Goldman says, driving it up to the cottage on the weekend, you should come out sometime, bring Cynthia and the girl, what's her name again? Hannah, he says, watching the moon paint the glass of neighbouring bank towers. The wind is cold. Of course, says Phil, embarrassed, perhaps, to have forgotten his boss's daughter's name, not noticing that his boss is indifferent, is preoccupied by moon and glass. What time is it, he wonders. When can I leave. Will the streets be quiet when I drive home. Will my mind be tranquil —and Phil's asking him if he'd like another drink. He says: thanks, scotch.

Phil heads to the bar, procures two glasses of scotch. Before he returns, he detours to the guardrail at the edge of the building, where there stands a woman in black. Her necklace is bright blue, and her earrings. You can see them at a distance. They stand out against the white of her skin. Phil greets her, smiles, gestures loosely with the glasses in his hands. She responds politely, he can see from across the roof, but not with feeling. She doesn't meet Phil's eye, rather stares off, much as he, Jake, stares off, at the city lit up and darkened in the night. He's never seen her before. Her hair is black. Her skin is pale. She looks, and he's not typically given to thoughts like this, thoughts touched by fancy, but the impression comes strongly: she looks like a swan. Long neck. Pink in the face, the cheeks pink, the lips pink, a softness and lightness about her beneath which you sense, as you sense in the presence of swans, a feral power. Phil laughs, touches her shoulder, rubs the finger vised tight by his wedding band against the side of his leg; she's remote, elsewhere. He watches. Hannah had a piano recital today. He missed it. He was in meetings, then at dinner with Steyn, a fund manager he likes, then at this party. No chance to see his daughter play, just time enough to call and hope to hear her voice, and find she'd gone into the theatre already, his wife wishing him well and telling him in her warm and charming way about her day's banal adventures with the not-for-profit board on which she volunteers, this grey Thursday's engagement. He watches the woman in black.

Phil returns, glasses in hand. They discuss a fraught merger in which the firm's involved, a problematic tributary of its paper trail that leads to a Chinese magnate connected to the Thai sex trade. He wants to laugh, wildly, dangerously. At a lull in their conversation, Phil glances at the woman in black, half laughs, half scowls. What a fucking nutcase, Phil says. Who, he says. You don't know about Rebecca Weiss? Why, he says, should I? Phil laughs. Secretary with Clearwater. Long story. Gross story. Beneath my dignity to gossip. Ask anyone on the seventh floor.

He approaches her. She leans against the guardrail, facing the city. He stands beside her and watches the city and drinks. I don't believe we've met, he says. You have a short memory, she says. I've got an excellent memory. Almost as excellent as your Latin dance — and it comes back to him, a charity function, a salsa band, they were introduced by George Massey, she asked him to dance, and when he danced with what he considered restraint, she ran a nail along the back of his neck and said: It's not a waltz, you know. I remember now, he says, forgive me, I try to repress my misguided attempts at grace. You shouldn't be talking to me, she says. Oh no? It'll be bad for business. Is that so. Don't look now, but everyone's staring at us. You have eyes in the back of your head? You're a good host, Mr. White, I appreciate that you want me to feel welcome, but I'd hate to deprive your more important guests of their star. My associate tells me you work at Clearwater, I'm surprised we haven't met before. I'm inconsequential, she says. Not like you. The new figure-head. He can't tell if she's being sincere. And he can't take his eyes off her. Congratulations on climbing to the very top rung, she says. I'd get vertigo.

A hand on his shoulder. Phil Goldman's there, with a short bald man he recognizes, a lawyer, Jenkins, Jones. An introduction is made and he's led away. He drinks, half-listens to Jenkins or Jones, nods and smiles, emits warmth. He thinks about his wife. Wise and kind, Jew-ish also, as he supposes this Rebecca Weiss must be. You might even say there's a resemblance, though not in the eyes, and not in the pallor, and not in the lips. They haven't had sex in six months. Since he was promoted, since he got the top job, to be exact. It's his fault more than hers. He's been busy, he's been tired. That's not why. He has felt, since he was promoted, an unease at home. He's stopped meeting his wife's eye. His daughter's too. He is aware of a stirring within himself of what he can only call shame. It bewilders him. He's developed a hab-it of leaving the house in the mornings before Cynthia and Hannah wake up. He slips out of bed, shaves and showers and dresses, skips coffee, skips breakfast. He used to love to see his wife and daughter at the kitchen table in the morning, it reminded him why he works, gave meaning to his labour. Now he feels an awkwardness even at the thought of it. He would sit with them and not know what to say. He'd feel like a stranger among them.

It's past one. The party's finished, the roof almost clear, the caterers putting lids on platters, wiping up. He says goodbye to Phil and friends and watches them go out, and turns to see Rebecca Weiss by herself at a table, her eyes on him. Still here, he says. Nowhere to go. Awfully well-dressed for a homeless person. Didn't say I'm homeless, she says without a smile, just got nowhere to go. Nowhere worth going. It happens sometimes: attend a party, stay till the end, meet no one interesting or no one available, then find at the end of the night I've got nowhere to go. And I can't go to sleep. Why not? I've lost the habit, it's like anything else, you don't sleep for long enough you lose the habit, you can't remember how once you did it so naturally, you try to recall the steps you took to fall asleep, what it felt like to stop thinking. Who are you, he says. She laughs. I imagine your wife must be very beautiful, she says, laughing. Yes she is. Go home, she says. And repeats, unaccountably: Go home, go home, go home. No, he says.

They leave together. She lives in a condo by the lake. He abandons his car in the parking garage and together they walk towards the water. Taxis' lights glare and pass by. The wind whistles through concrete. He feels as though in a dream. Their words, their glances, their syncopated steps — about it all is a lightness, as though nothing they do together could possibly be of any consequence. How crazy that is. He knows, he knows. She'll invite him inside, he knows. And then what. He has made no firm decision about this, though he's got presence of mind enough to realize that to walk this far at her side is probably itself a decision. He's always been faithful to his wife. He's never been seriously tempted. Even now,

even strolling alongside this woman with blue necklace
against white collarbone, even this doesn't feel like temp-
tation, feels rather like a game. Their not talking about it,
their drifting down the windy street together in silence
— this is the complicity of children who each know the
rules to a game but won't speak them aloud, lest by speaking they prove that their game is manmade and not magic.
How drunk are they? Just barely. She's beautiful to him,
but no more so than his wife, and not conventionally so,
not an ideal, too strange, too fierce. Who's leading, he
wonders. Did I will this or did she? Do I have the power
to stop it? And do I want it to stop?

   When they get to her building, she invites him in.
He comes in. Their clothes are on the floor right away.
When they're finished he asks if he can have a glass of
water. She disappears into the kitchen and he thinks:
I'm now a man who does this. Then he thinks, just as
distinctly, with surprise: And I'm not ashamed. Which
isn't to say he's proud, either, he doesn't see the evening
in terms of conquest, and anyway he's not sure whether
she'd be his conquest or he hers, but gone now is the
feeling of shame that plagues him at home, in the office,
as he sits in traffic, the sense that he's lost direction, that
something hard and fast in his soul has dissolved just
lately and he doesn't know how it's happened and he
doesn't know how to make himself whole again. He feels
happy. Thirsty. Their sex was satisfying. He likes the
sound of her in her kitchen. The view from her bedroom,
the wide, dark sweep of the lake. She returns with his
water and stands by the bedside, in the glow of a lamp

he's turned on. Her curves delight him. Her hair falls across her breasts. Thank you, he says. She nods, distant, and withdraws to the balcony. Who are you, he says. She turns and he sees that she's crying. I don't mean to be rude, but you should go, she says.

He drives home, morning comes, and so does guilt. But he can't stop thinking about her. In bed beside his sleeping wife he thinks about her. At his desk, in meetings, watching numbers diminish, increase, he thinks about her. He imagines he sees her face at crowded crosswalks, in the parking garage, behind an elevator's closing doors. He gets little work done. After lunch he buzzes Paulson, a young analyst, hardworking and discreet, whom his predecessor lured from Clearwater Capital, the firm where she works. He's always liked Paulson. Narcissism, maybe: Paulson reminds him of himself, what he might've been at thirty had he been in this business then. Have a seat, he says casually as Paulson eases the door shut behind him. Tell me, what do you know about Rebecca Weiss? Paulson blinks. What, you mean the dirt?

It's all gossip. To be taken with a grain of salt, says Paulson, and frankly I'd take the whole shaker. Goes something like this, she's on vacation, Venice, two or three weeks, she meets a guy, English, and they fall hard for each other, they have a thing. So what happens is I guess she decides this romance is more important than what she's left behind here, because she doesn't come home, she follows this guy back to London, and they're shacked up for I don't know, a month or two. Anyway, here comes the crazy part. Mitch Friedman at Clearwater, he's in London meeting clients. He gets out of the Tube and who does he see in Hyde Park, on a bench by herself, but our lady. He tries to talk to her. And what does she do, she ignores him. Completely. Acts like he isn't there at all. He makes some calls, I don't know the details exactly, but apparently she's had some sort of breakdown, she's an outpatient at a hospital over there. Two weeks later, Monday morning she shows up for work downstairs as if nothing's happened. Everybody goes what the fuck, right? But she seems totally fine, you'd never know anything weird had gone down. And nobody wants an HR hassle, so we all kind of nod and go oh, okay. And that's it. And then a couple days later she disappears again. Make some calls, eventually they call her building manager, building manager knocks on her door, she's at home. She's just decided not to show up for work again. A guy from Clearwater goes over to her place to talk to her, she's civil and everything, invites our guy in, offers him coffee, but when he asks her why she's not at the office she shrugs and says she can't get out of bed. You're out of bed now, our guy says. I can't get out the front door, she says, I know it's unacceptable, you should probably fire me. Crazy, right? She was never like this before, back when I knew her. Sweet, sexy, sharp wit. Dude did a real number on her when he dumped her.

He's flirting with danger, he knows, but he can't turn his face from it, he feels mesmerized, eyes fixed to a flame burning up in an unknown dark. Daylight floods his office, feels cloying. He leaves early, considers going to see her, decides against it. At home in the afternoon, his wife out on errands, his daughter at school, he sits in his study with the lights off, watches the arms of his old apple tree sway in the breeze. He stares at his bookshelf, lingers over his several editions of *Anna Karenina*. He thinks not about Vronsky and Anna's adulterous passion, as if in search of instructive parallels, but instead about Levin, the man who wins all that he desires — beautiful young wife, tranquil domesticity, a life of genteel leisure — only to find his thoughts turn again and again to the razorblade, the pistol, the noose. A man prosperous and lost. Worried his irreverent life has meant nothing and yet unable to turn to religion, unable to believe. He hears his daughter come home, move about. He likes to listen to her like this, in her private moments. She's come from choir practice, he remembers. Friday. A committed girl, his daughter, to stay after school to sing on a Friday, the weekend awaiting. Committed, focused, a real go-getter. Like him, like her father: destined for big things, for success, like her father. He sits in his study and listens, not making a sound.

After work on Monday, he returns to Rebecca's apartment. She buzzes him in, meets him at the door without surprise. Their sex is fierce, fraught. She makes coffee. You shouldn't have come back, she says as they sit together in her narrow kitchen, coffees steaming. I understand I'm a great adventure, but look at me. You must know about me. Now that we've done this once or twice, isn't it time you got back to your perfectly ordered life? You have a distorted image of me, he says. She laughs. Describe your wife to me. Give me a break. Please, I'm curious, I want

to picture her, I think about her all the time, she's become a central figure in my daydreams, I want to get the
picture right. Your wife, your house, your little family.
What do you do here all day, he says, you should get out
of the apartment, I understand this guy hurt you, but—
her chair scrapes linoleum, she moves to the cupboard,
takes a bottle of bourbon down from the shelf. Come
for a walk with me, he says. Your wife will see us. Let's get
dinner. What do you want from me, she says. He's silent.
Her apartment is bright, swept with the day's last daylight. I feel rude when I kick you out after sex, she says,
and I hate to be rude, so maybe let's end this here. Fine,
he says.

 That's it. It's over. He's sad, he's relieved, a bit bewildered. But soon he slips back into his accustomed patterns. Work consumes his attention, distracts him. He becomes once again an attentive husband and loving father, remembers how to play those parts convincingly, smooth
out the wrinkles, plaster over the gaps through which
peek inadmissible desires, unhelpful questions. One night
later that week, when he's sure Hannah's asleep, he crosses the hall to Cynthia's bedroom. (They've long slept in
separate rooms, first because he snored, later, after his
snoring abruptly stopped, because they were already in
the habit and why break the habit when it works so well
for them both, affords them such rest.) She's reading,
something about the Jewish population in British Man-
datory Palestine. His smile is wry. Should I be concerned
about this? She sets the book on her knee. Just because
you like to pretend you have no history and no roots

doesn't mean everyone else has to, she says. He kisses her. He kisses her again. Honey, she says. You don't want to? I want to, sure, but … you're not too tired? I'm wide awake, he says.

It's good. He thinks this during the act and afterwards. It's *better*. His affair was a flop by comparison. Cynthia's attentive, present, she knows what pleases him, he knows what pleases her and he's pleased by her pleasure; while with Rebecca—enigmatic, unknown, an adventure (to use her word)—he was ungenerous, thought only of his own hunger and how to sate it. He liked himself less with her. Was it a mistake, he wonders, picturing Rebecca's narrow, harrowed face in the shadows of his darkened bedroom as he returns from his wife. No, not a mistake. It was, he might say, at the risk of rationalist glibness, an enriching experience. Not dignified, but nevertheless a contribution to the fabric of his life, to his understanding of the world and of himself, a garish light that reveals to him the boundaries of the role he plays, where lies the line beyond which he becomes, irrevocably, another man. The womanizer. The erotic man of influence, proud and insatiable. Even Voltaire, he remembers, wouldn't reject sexual intrigue if wisdom were at stake, Voltaire who slept with a man once for the sake of philosophy but wouldn't repeat the experiment. He's had his moment. And he's glad that it's passed.

A week later he wakes up so depressed he can hardly get out of bed. It takes him an hour to dress. He's late for work, he's unshaven. His colleagues notice; he doesn't care. Shame twists him again, again he's consumed by thoughts of her, long neck, pink cheeks. Yet how absurd that is! He doesn't love her, he hardly respects her, she leads the sort of shadowy life he rejected as an undergraduate, as vapid as lurid. He has more than she does, he has everything. So why does he scan her file over and over, obsess for hours about their time together, the sound of her voice? He comes to the conclusion, by the end of this black day, that he's sorry for her, profoundly sorry, that this funk he's in is subconscious penance for the luck he's had, the happiness she's been deprived of. He realizes he wants to help her, give to her; his love for her, if love it is, is basically philanthropic; or perhaps all love is. (No, he thinks: no, all love isn't.) They must be close to the same age, maybe she's a bit younger, but he realizes he thinks of her almost like a daughter. He wants to offer her friendship. He wants to offer himself as a salve.

Cheered and purposeful, nervous, he returns to her apartment after work. I'll leave if you want me to, he says as she opens the door. I just want to see how you are. Her eyes are raccooned with fatigue. I've got the kettle on, she says, you want tea? And she steps out of the doorway. They sit in her kitchen and talk. He finds it difficult to say what he means, what he's resolved to say. I want to see you, he says; which isn't what he means. She's pale. I don't know if I can do this. Not like we've been doing. I want to see you as a friend, a companion. You've come back to reject me? I've come back because I think you need me in your life. She laughs. Call me arrogant. Arrogant, yes. And I need you in mine. Like a shot in the head, she says, laughing. It seems to me you must spend too much time here by yourself. What do you do with your days? I read, she says. I read about the irremediable loneliness of the soul, it's the only kind of reading that makes me laugh, and I like to laugh. I masturbate, I surf the Internet. I look at pictures of places I once travelled. Most of them have changed since I was there. It makes me feel old. A feeling I like. And I write, she says. Really. Yes. I can show you. And she rises and drifts into the living room, her shoulders slumped, her walk languid.

She's written poetry. Reams of it. He sits beside her on the sofa and reads from a battered notebook, her gaze hot on his cheek. He has no idea why she's opened up to him, shared with him these intimate stirrings laid out in chicken scratch, but he doesn't question it. He's glad of it. Well? she says. He keeps reading. Much of her writing is histrionic, verbose. But some is extraordinary. A poem about a street brawl outside the apartment where she lived with her lover in London, her feeling then of the fragility of her world's order, how swiftly violence breaks out, the equally jarring swiftness with which it ends, and the silence it leaves. A poem about strangers' children: longing for them in Covent Garden, considering what the theft of a child would entail, if it might be defensible. Many about her lover. All of her interesting poems, he finds, are in some way connected to that man, London or Venice, sudden departures. Your opinion is loaded, she says, I know your credentials. Does she refer to his aborted career as a scholar? To his own

youthful attempts at verse, published in prominent jour-
nals, promising, abandoned, scuttled by his feeling that
poetry isn't a craft, can't be perfected, admits only fail-
ure in finer and finer degrees, perpetuating the illusion
that something permanent might in the last event be
said? It's good, he says. Do you still write? No, he says,
haven't for a long time. Why not? Never really liked to.
I found words weren't well suited to express the way I
saw the world, words specify, make concrete, I stopped
writing because I felt my experience of the world was less
stable than that, constantly shifting, a series of impres-
sions none of them trustworthy neither evil nor good, I
found words pinned things down too rigidly, so I stopped.
Numbers are better, at least the numbers I deal with, they
don't claim to explain the world, only their own world-
ly sphere, transient, limited. She stares at him, runs her
hands through his hair. I painted, he says. Late adolescence. I painted constantly. That was better. Suited me
better. I thought that was what I'd do with my life. Why
didn't you? The lifestyle. The form of life. It scared me.
Get up, sit down and work, eat drink sleep. And again.
No sense of advancing, progressing, rising. I was scared
I would feel I were standing still all my life. She places
her finger on his lips, traces the edge of his lips with her
nail. So?

He must be a better husband and father. As he emerges from her building into an evening sun shower, her
scent lingering faintly, he decides this. It's clear that the
affair will go on, he's too weak to end it and doesn't want
to, it makes him happy, it calms him: but it also creates

a debt, and he must pay it. He won't leave his wife. What eases and delights him, he sees clearly, is not the affair but the balance, the harmonics of family and lover struck together, routine redeemed by voluptuous escape. There's a careers fair approaching at Hannah's school, and he volunteers, with Hannah's blessing, to speak about business and banking and markets in terms that 13-year-olds can understand. He shows up, makes jokes, stokes dreams. Afterwards he takes Hannah out for lunch. Are there a lot of girl investment bankers, she asks him over teriyaki chicken. Some, he says. I think I want to do that, she says. I want to be like you, if I can get better at math. He laughs. You don't need much math to do what I do. Then what do you need? I don't know, he says. Luck. Instincts. Appetite.

Most evenings, when he arrives home from Rebecca's apartment at dusk, he takes his wife and daughter for dinner, listens with pleasure to their laughter, stories of their day. And later at night, most nights, silence reigning in the wide halls of their immaculate, under-furnished house in Forest Hill, he slips into Cynthia's room and they make love. One night, as they finish, he sees she's crying. His stomach drops; somehow she's found out. What is it, he asks. I didn't get a chance to know you when you were young, she says. When you were twenty. Somebody else got that. Another woman. And tonight I thought: this is what he was like. He finds himself moved also. Shattered, for a moment. But he covers it up, catches his breath, swallows hard. So I was doing it like a boy? I was fumbling? No. And you know it. I'm still in love with you, she says. Oh. Was that in question? I didn't ask the question, I'm very good at not asking those questions, but tonight I did and the answer is I'm still in love with you. Good. Good, I'm glad. And you, she asks. Are you still in love with me, Jake? It was never a question for me, he says.

It's humid and grey early summer when the call about the suicide attempt wakes him in the night. Thought you'd like to know, says Paulson, thought you wouldn't want to be the last to know. She's at Mount Sinai, she's been admitted. He flies out of the house, his shoes half on. Driving down empty side streets, he has the distinct sensation of falling. She's unconscious when he gets there, nobody at her bedside. He asks a nurse what happened. Are you family? Close friend. Pills, says the nurse. She'll be fine. In the short term at least. Are you staying with her? She's been alone all night. He sits by her for hours, watches her chest rise and fall. Every few minutes he has to fight the urge to lean over the bed and shake her, hard. She wakes around seven, doesn't react to the sight of him. Maybe she doesn't recognize me, he thinks. Maybe she wasn't trying to kill herself, maybe she was trying to scrub her memory clean, maybe it's worked. You're going to be late to the office, she says. He's silent. Her eyes fixed on the ceiling, she shakes her head. I'm a lark. An itch. It means nothing. You'll never leave your wife. We're killing time. I won't love again. I've tried, I've tried and I've tried and I've tried and I've tried, and I can't. It isn't in me, it's dead, I can't. And I don't want to pretend anymore.

The affair barrels downhill from there. They fight terribly the day after she returns home. A vase smashed, chairs overturned. Minutes after he leaves her apartment, he can no longer remember what the fight was about. He swears to forget her, promises himself it's over this time for good. Late evening now and the streets are still crowded, streams of strangers milling towards subway entrances, men and women in suits leaving work, and young people, so many kids, holding hands and stealing kisses. What are they doing here, so deep downtown, in the smog of trade? He slows, watches them, tries to remember what he wanted at that age; tries to remember what he wanted yesterday. He's tempted to descend into the subway tunnels with them, to retreat underground, anonymous, and disappear.

But he must get rice. Cynthia's asked him to pick some up. She's cooking tonight, stir-fry chicken. A meal he likes. Too much drama, he thinks, not good. Bad blood pressure in the family. He retrieves his car from beneath his office tower, heads north, home. Dusk is settling already and traffic's light.

~

A week later he hears from his brother for the first time in ten years. He's on his back porch on a muggy Sunday afternoon when Cynthia hands him the phone, and from the look on her face he guesses it's Ezra even before the first word rasps over the line from Vancouver. Jake, Jake. Been way too long. Good to hear your voice,

man. His brother makes small talk: I heard about the
crazy weather out there, like a sauna, hot here too this
year but you know Vancouver, not so suffocating, can't
stand that. Ezra asks about Cynthia and Hannah, about
work: Still trading stocks for millionaires, huh, got any
hot tips for me? He answers perfunctorily—his girls are
fine, no hot tips, everything's fine. The porch door slides
open behind him and Hannah emerges, a slim volume
of poetry tucked under her arm. She crosses the backyard into the shade of the apple tree and sits, absorbed
at once. He realizes he's been silent on the line and so
has Ezra. So, says Ezra. He waits. So, I … I'm not just
calling to shoot the shit, I know you probably don't …
He waits. You're not in touch with dad, huh. No, he says,
not lately. He's … fuck, Jake, I'm out on a limb here, I
don't know what to do with this, I love you. Okay? I
love you. What's going on, he says. The phone's damp
now with sweat, the heat unbearable. He's got maybe a
few days, man. Asshole, you know? To go and get like
this. Mom called me, you know Mom, said she refused
to call you if I wouldn't, she was doing her old thing,
trying to get you and me … anyway, the point is he's got
maybe a few days and … well, as you can imagine … Silence. Finally, quiet but resolved: I'm not going to see
him. Thought about it. But the answer is no. Gotta be
that way. And maybe one of us should go. So. I know it's
pressure and everybody'd understand if you couldn't
come out, you're all the way across the fucking contin-
ent, it's an interruption, I know that, but anyway, there
it is. Up to you. Take care of yourself. I love you, man.

The sun is shining, birds are singing, his daughter is reading beneath the shade of the apple tree, and on his back and neck the sweat is rapidly chilling. He shivers and goes into the house. Upstairs in his bedroom, he shuts the door and swears till he wears himself out. Unsteady, a tightness in his chest, he yanks a suitcase from the closet, unzips it and throws it open on the floor, flings clothing in. He must be loud, because Cynthia appears in the doorway. She asks him what's happened, where he's going. Vancouver, he says. He packs. Don't let him, she says. Don't let him what. Whatever he's doing this time. Whatever he's asking you for. Don't give in. He keeps packing. He knows he's not being fair to her — she wants only to help, to understand. But he's unable to offer any coherent account of what he feels right now. I have a fundraising meeting at the synagogue tonight, please get dinner for Hannah before you go, she says as she leaves the room, her voice edged with exasperation. He keeps packing.

On the flight west he imagines what he'll say to his father and what his father will say to him. It'll be difficult, he thinks as he gazes at the ridged seafloor of clouds. They've always had trouble communicating. His father was once a king of the garment industry, in charge of three factories and an army of salesmen that he'd inherited from his own father, who'd built the business nearly from scratch, so the family mythology goes, after escaping pogroms in Poland with pocket change and forged papers. And his father directed the interests of this dynasty for many years, shortly before and after the death

of his own father, and the family was prosperous, and
Jake idolized his father, not only because the family was
prosperous but also because his father seemed, even to a
boy of twelve, a complete person, the image of balance and
grace, kind and loving to his family, wise about matters
both high and low. When accusations surfaced of his
father's embezzlement of funds, he felt no scorn, felt only
that a time of great difficulty approached and they should
prepare themselves for it. He was right. His father lost
everything. And one morning he woke up and was an
adolescent and his father seemed to him a humiliated
man, and this wasn't just the typical disenchantment of
adolescence but also true. His father retreated into drink
and self-pity; at thirteen, fifteen, eighteen, he saw this and
didn't know how to feel, swung from hatred to wrench-
ing sympathy. They drifted together and apart with the
seasons while he still lived at his parents' house, he never
arrived at the settled hostility towards his father that
Ezra, still a child then, soon developed, but they never
spoke as easily as they'd done before, especially not after
he adopted his mother's Anglo-Saxon maiden name, White
—a name, to his mind, innocent of history, free of remembered mythology or tradition, a name he could in-
scribe as he wished—as the standard he bore into the
world.

He lands in Vancouver late at night and takes a cab
to the hospital. The nurse on duty tells him his father is
asleep, hasn't stirred much all day. His father's condition
is precarious but, for the moment, stable. He glances into
the room and turns away. I'll come back in the morning.

He leaves his hotel details at the nurse's station, requests that he be contacted immediately if anything changes.

From his hotel room, he calls Ezra to tell him that he's come. He makes a token suggestion to meet at the hospital the next morning, which Ezra ignores. They settle on breakfast at the hotel restaurant. When they hang up he undresses, goes to the window, peers out. It's dark now and all he can see are lights in the harbour and on the North Shore. In the morning the mountains will greet him. If even a little he believes in God, mountains have something to do with it. On previous trips to Vancouver, he's had the thought more than once that they're appointed here as guardians of his father and brother, that they perform the sacred filial, fraternal duty that he's impiously shirked. Yet the sleep he falls into is warm and fathomless.

In the morning, in the lobby, he spots Ezra right away, at a window table in the hotel restaurant, coffee mug and newspaper in front of him. He's aged. And groomed to deny it: long hair, scruff, T-shirt and jeans. Self-conscious about his pressed shirt and pants, he goes into the restaurant and greets his brother. Ezra stumbles to his feet, grins, extends his hand. Good to see your face, hasn't changed a bit. Yours neither. Ezra asks again about Cynthia and Hannah, his house, his job. Still the happiest man alive, aren't you? Things are fine, he says. He's about to ask after Ezra's wife, but Ezra pre-empts him: Yeah, Sheila and I fucked it up years ago, after my troubles, she stayed with me for a while but when my luck ran out and the cash was gone and I couldn't provide for her lifestyle, well. I'm sorry, he says, I didn't know. No no, of course, it was all happening a long ways away from you. Ezra flags the waiter and orders a glass of rye. A bit early, I know, he says, but a little before lunchtime calms my nerves, I don't make a habit of it, I'm under a lot of pressure, and it's a, how would you say, a special occasion. His drink arrives. Cheers. Can I persuade you to come to the hospital with me? Ezra sets the glass down. He frowns, his eyes wander. Nah, he says. Not interested. Wish it were different, but the thing is, I know it won't make anyone happy, not me, not him, you know? All it'll do is make me feel like shit, and he'll be no better off, either. No better off, he thinks, in a final sense, maybe, but he knows their father would be struck by how uncannily Ezra has grown into the old man's echo. Macho, fragile. Pretentious about lack of pretention, wielding lack of affectation affectedly, like a challenge. And hot-blooded: quick to anger, quick to love, betrayal intolerably keen. Sorry. Wish I felt otherwise. In other news, says Ezra, I've got a business prospect that could be real interesting, we should talk, we always said we'd get into something together. And Ezra outlines the details of a new industrial development along the oceanfront in Richmond. Investment possibilities. Let's talk more about it later, he says, and changes the subject. He eats quickly. As soon as he can, he says he has to get going, he's meeting a client in West Vancouver before he returns to the hospital. It isn't true, and he lies badly, too emphatically, but the pull his brother has always had on his life's orbit is insidious. Good to see your face, Ezra

says. Let's meet up again before you head home. Talk
business.

He walks across town to the beach, watches boats drift
into the bay. From here his life back home looks strange
and small. His time with Rebecca Weiss feels from this
distance like a pebble dropped into the centre of the ocean,
a brief ripple testifying to the impact, then nothing. The
objects of his life back east seem featureless. He can remember his house's size and colour, say, but details elude
him: how close together the hedges are, the shape of the
doorknobs, what's tacked to the fridge. His wife's face,
the face of his child — of course he never forgets them.
But from this distance their edges are blurred. At moments
like these, anonymous in the ocean breeze, he remembers that he existed before those others existed in his life.

It's nearly evening when he works up the nerve to
cross the threshold of his father's hospital room. He sits
bedside for an hour before his father wakes, senses his
presence, turns to face him. They haven't seen each other
in a year, since his father last flew east to visit his grand-
daughter, stayed at their house for a week during the
summer and complained about draughty windows.
Looks about the same now. Faded. You must be jetlagged,
the old man says, his voice all catch and rasp. His father's concentration isn't good, and he seems to be hallu-
cinating, refers a few times to "the bunch of you," others
in the room. The old man asks after Hannah, Cynthia.
They're fine, he says. He mentions Hannah's excellent
marks, the high school where she'll start in the fall. His
father drifts out of consciousness again.

The night wears on. He wanders out to the nurses' station and talks to a nurse about his father's condition, returns to the room, reads yesterday's paper. He's standing by the window at around two in the morning when the old man opens his eyes and speaks in a tremulous voice he almost doesn't recognize. No, not me, I was too good for that, I never went to *shul*, I never went to church with your mother, oh no, I thought it was bullshit, I paraded that around the house, hypocrisy, let the fools pray, what do I need with cheap consolation. As if I knew anything. Maybe it would've helped. Tell your mother I regret everything. Tell your brother I forgive him and God help him.

His father dies in his sleep a few hours later. He calls Cynthia, who offers condolences and to get on a plane with Hannah; he asks them to stay put. Easier that way. The cemetery isn't far from the beach and the scent of the ocean permeates the proceedings, he's aware of it acutely, it distracts him. Ezra isn't there. He consoles his mother. She and his father divorced twenty years ago, she'd been involved with Lionel for many years more than that, the affair open and acknowledged, Lionel the real paternal force in the house after his father's fall. But it's clear that she's shaken. Lionel's dead, and she's drifted from her children. She must feel terribly alone, he knows, and the thought of it saddens him, but the truth is that she's become a stranger to him. His feeling towards her is respectful and obliging yet also disturbingly cool. He accompanies her to her hotel after the funeral and proposes they have dinner together so she won't be by herself. She says she'll call to let him know. He knows she won't.

He returns to his own hotel room and repacks his suitcase, restores items to his toiletry kit. When he's finished, he calls Ezra and tells him that their father is buried. Ezra is silent on the line, and then he weeps and weeps and tries to talk and can't and so keeps weeping. He listens to his brother cry, breathes into the line to let him know he's there. I'm leaving tonight, he says. Thank you for letting me know he was almost out of time. I'm glad I came. I'm glad I saw you. There's a long silence. He notices his brother's breathing has changed, acquired a sharpness. Like the last time. He has a presentiment of what's coming and he's right. You fucker, says Ezra. You bloodless trash. Why don't you fuck off and die. Not hesitating but not angry, he hangs up. He falls back on the bed, sets the alarm for a few hours later, early evening, and sinks into sleep.

Later he'll wonder what might have happened if instead he'd checked out early. If he hadn't been there to receive the call from reception, to hear Paulson whisper the news. He'll wonder if, had he called Cynthia with his plane's arrival time in Toronto, he might've been on the other line when Paulson tried to reach him. Later there will be days when he wishes this is what had happened. He'll imagine his wife's face grown older, folds of skin on her neck slackened with age. He'll struggle to remember the way his house looked when he approached it at dusk in the evenings, on his way home from work or Rebecca, and how far apart the hedges were, and the shape of the doorknobs, and the shine of Cynthia's auburn hair in sunlight, in the kitchen. All this could still have been mine, he'll think. I have given up my inheritance to venture forth into the wilderness and I do not know what fortune awaits me there, perhaps only death awaits me. Nevertheless I have packed my bag with those few things I require and I will not ask for anything while I live though I may want so help me God. Was this his cast of mind in those first moments? Later he won't be able to recall. And he'll worry that his actions then were not a poem but merely animal. Instinct, survival.

The ring of the phone on the nightstand penetrates a dream of dunes and wakes him around 4:30. He feels groggy, bleary-eyed, he sits up, nausea. Phone knocked from its cradle, retrieved off the floor, raised to his throbbing head—yeah? A call for you from Toronto, sir. Yeah, okay. And there's Paulson, whispering, asking him how his flight was, how his trip's been, not getting to the point. Unlike him. Why are you whispering? He sits on the edge of the bed, nauseous, thirsty. Okay, says Paulson, I can tell you everything at once or I can let you deal with one thing at a time. Tell me everything at once. She's dead. No screwing around this time. Knife through the heart. I'm very sorry. It knocks the wind out of him. When his breath returns, it brings with it the taste of vomit. The other part you need to know, says Paulson telling him everything at once, is she left a note, going through her reasons, making her argument for suicide and so on, a lot of garbage, she was a very sick lady, but you need to know that even though she doesn't use your name, you're mentioned in it. In a way that might be problematic. What does she say? Well, she says, more or less, that there's a man in her life who — Read it to me. Paulson hesitates. Sound of a briefcase unfastened, papers riffled. *Don't want to keep rolling my numb body up the hill each day. Can't. Won't. Too heavy. Longing for the man I can't have. Pity for the other one. Good God. This man has won everything in his life by exertion of the will and he values none of it. His wife is a possession, his daughter is a weekend hobby. His life is perfectly rational, perfectly controlled, perfectly meaningless to him. He's incapable of genuine passion, he has eliminated from his life the possibility of anything transcendent, for the sake of simplicity, and out of fear. He'd be a narcissist if he weren't such a coward, as it is he's desperately afraid to look at himself, I think he must avoid mirrors for fear of finding he has no reflection. He'll believe I'm killing myself because I'm miserable, but he's wrong. I'm killing myself out of love. Because there's nothing in the world but love and probably nothing out of the world but love either. I've exhausted my options here. I will take my chances elsewhere.*

The first thing he does after hanging up the phone is unzip his bag and let its contents spill across the floor.

II.

He had a child's wonder. Beyond fifty and grey and ragged and his eyes were a child's and he listened as though he were certain each stranger might offer a revelation that would upset his vision of the world. He was terribly lonely. He had not one month before committed an act of terrible defiance and it nearly killed him, but when I met him he was beginning to emerge from the shadow of what he'd done. He had but a day earlier come forth from the woods where he'd been camping. I call it camping. He'd been sleeping in the woods, that's all. He'd carried in his sack a paltry amount of food and water, he'd had no knowledge of those woods or of wilderness survival, and if a bear had come or some other misfortune had befallen him, he would have been helpless. How he occupied himself in those days, half-buried in silence, I can't say. What peace he knew was mixed with staggering pain, the cost of his act of terrible defiance. But just imagine him then: this man who'd spent his life in a grey tower then come down and lived each hour upon the black earth.

I spied on him. Daily he rose late, dressed quickly, left the inn without eating and traipsed through the woods to the beach. I took my lunch break when he left and followed him, and when he emerged on the beach I hid behind the rocks and observed his ritual. He stripped naked. Naked he waded into the water, and in the blistering light he bathed himself and sounds emerged from him that were not song but were not speech either. He was calling his ships to return to him. What those ships were and what bounty they carried neither I nor likely he himself could say. He was exulting in his freedom and trying to exorcise the demons his freedom brought or did not purge. After he had thus bathed himself he returned to the beach and lay down in the sand and there in the caustic sunlight typical of that summer he lingered.

Jacob's isolated corner of beach was significant to me moreover because it was there that as a girl my life was changed by Wilson Nash. In my last year of high school Wilson Nash was my boyfriend. That was the time when I began to hear my voices. Sometimes woman and sometimes man, my voices from the start issued instructions. They commanded trivial things in those early days: don't eat that potato, lift your left foot three times before you enter the church on Sunday, that sort of thing. Now I can see those tasks were tests. There were intimations of purpose in my voices' first commands, but forceful revelation of my purpose was to come much later, when I was ready for it. In the beginning my voices only impressed on me that I must do as they said.

That night on the beach when I was seventeen, Wilson grew amorous and I had to tell him what my loudest voice, the shrill female one, had told me, that I was to leave him and forget about him as soon as I could manage it. This struck him as a declaration of unfathomable cruelty. He was confused and angry and felt something was owed him. I resisted at first but soon ceased to protest, aware that a purpose lay in wait for me that no act of brutality could interfere with. It wasn't long before the town knew of what they called my madness. The story of my rape became known also and transmuted into the story of my promiscuity, more palatable than the rape of the mad and requiring no involvement of the law. My family bore the social cost as much as I did.

Nobody acknowledged the genuine reason why a penalty was thus exacted.

Within days of Jacob's arrival at the inn, I began to receive from my voices intimations of his importance. At first only hints I got, keep an eye on that man, have you noticed the way he walks, the quality of his gaze, pay attention. My shrill voice soon grew more pointed. That man is your deliverance and you are his, it told me. And so I sought to know him better. One morning at the beach where he swam naked daily, I shed my clothes and stepped out from my hiding place to meet him in my nakedness. It was a rather silly while before he noticed, and when finally he did he was a ways out in the water and I think he didn't quite trust his eyes, because as he crept to shore he betrayed no reaction at all. We observed each other at ten paces. Without a word between us, I came to him and he took me in his arms. He lowered our bodies to the sand. The midday sun was hot upon us and the tongue of the ocean needled our embrace. But he surprised me then and merely held me close. I thought he must be repelled by my body. But as he gripped me tight the shame passed out of me, and I grew convinced that my purpose lay indeed with this man.

Our days wove themselves together. I'd follow him to the beach by mornings, my presence now acknowledged and plain and what a relief it was, to watch him with frankness, in my nakedness behold his. My senses woke, and all through my body coursed the rattle of the firs and maple leaves, the taste of the ocean breeze, the blue of the sky and the white of the spume and the long, browning flanks of Jacob's weathered body. He ploughed his limbs through the ragged water and made the noises I've described, not quite song but not speech either. Afterwards he'd lie with me, though we continued through that season to abstain. And more and more this seemed no insult and no loss, and more and more I sensed his importance. We lay there like animals scarred by a hunt narrowly escaped and not long past, nursing each other's wounds.

It wasn't till I found the courage to visit his room one evening after dinner that words came. He was reticent, but once I'd coaxed a first detail out of him, that his father had died, it would've been impossible to dam the flood that followed. When he spoke about the family he'd abandoned and his departure from them, he did so in a way that was contradictory, confused. He said he was in search of something. He didn't know what. He believed the manner of living he had abandoned was poisonous to him, though he could not say precisely why or with what form of life he hoped to replace it. Often there was an undertone suggesting that he saw his time in our town as a sort of temporary wilderness trial, a test of his resolve and of the willingness of the world to reveal the truths he sought. Often there was an undertone suggesting that to his family and his avowed amoral life he would soon return.

Yet it was only a month later that circumstances changed. He came in from the woods one day soaked through with rain and said he wished to renew a bad habit of his youth, and did I know a place in town where he could find rudimentary art supplies. I directed him

to a store that would suit his ends, where he bought canvases and an easel and paints of basic colours. These he
carried past the inn to the half-drowned woods. Absent
he remained for five hours. It was early evening when at
last he returned, the autumn sky streaked with dark. He
did not leave his room for dinner. The door was unlocked
when I arrived and that was strange, usually he locked
his door and checked his locks with a paranoid rigour.
I crept inside and found him seated on the far side of the
bed with the easel before him, its matter concealed from
me by the angle. He motioned that I should approach.

But it was no longer just the two of us in the room.
My voices erupted in a raging chorus and I doubled over
from the shock, he asked if I was okay, I could barely
hear him much less answer. It was some time before the
exhortations within me calmed enough that I could dis-
tinguish them. The shrill voice broke through at last
and told me Jacob was tied to the destiny of our race in
ways the greatness and terror of which it was beyond me
to conceive, and now my time had come to live my purpose, which was to see the fruits of that man's soul de-
livered into the light of day, where the impact they were
destined to have was greater and more awful than that
of the Hebrew prophets whose vision for mankind was
carried forth unto the nations past the bloodied thresh-
olds of disbelief, lo and behold, lo and behold, *that*. *That*
was my sacred calling. *That* belonged to me, Patricia
Bender, whom everybody sneered at and ignored and
thought a whore and an awful blasphemer wise to keep
the children far away from. The shrill voice spoke thus to

me. And it was a long time before the passion subsided and I became again aware of my body sprawled on Jacob's bed. The man loomed over me with a look on his face of considerable concern. What on earth could I say. I shook with terror that he'd spurn me for my strangeness. But he merely asked again if I was okay.

Soon afterwards, Jacob said he planned to leave our town and asked if I'd come with him. He'd met a man in the harbour who hoped to sell his cottage and Jacob had proffered the total sum in cash. I told him I'd join him. Gave me no pause. My voices continued to insist on his importance, and he and I had developed what could be called little other than a marriage. Chaste it was, yet I called forth from him the truest stuff of his heart, and he treated me with a tenderness so unlike the glares I'd known most of my life.

I never quit my job at the inn, just packed my bag and left with Jacob. He had purchased a vehicle from the man who'd sold him the cottage, and it was a cool October morning when into the back of that car we loaded the nothing the both of us owned and piled in and drove out of town. We had food for weeks and water and some tools the uses of which I knew even if Jacob didn't, such ignorance a comical remnant of his prior life. I'd been the one to prepare our provisions also. It was the beginning of a mutual reliance that was to blossom between Jacob and me, a partnership that left him free to become a man untouched by anything outside his immediate sphere. He spoke during our long drive of the needfulness of that transformation. He said he would live henceforward an apolitical life. I just kept my mouth shut. I knew that whatever the story he told himself about why we were driving out of sight of mankind, there to remain for years and perhaps for the rest of our lives, he was certain in that isolation to set upon work of great importance, and I was to be his succour and his aid, his midwife, his wife.

The sun was shining when we arrived at the place that was to be our home. We'd travelled there through the thick of the woods and it was evident on the last stretch of our drive that we'd ventured far from other human life. The property seemed a wreck. The clearing in which the house stood was overgrown with weeds, and through the tangles skittered small life in great profusion. The house itself boasted wood boards rotten past recovery, a dilapidated porch half crumbling, the stairs broken, the front door unwilling to close. Yet the interior suited our ends just fine. The rustic furnishings were in good repair, as were the windows, tall and broad. They flooded the house with light. Perhaps on account of the proliferation of dust that hung everywhere suspended in the sun, that light seemed not entirely of this world. The look on Jacob's face gave form to the pleasure I felt. He brushed dust off the kitchen table and plugged in the refrigerator and drew an age of repressed water from the tap. We slipped out of the house and roamed the edge of the woods and drank deep our wilderness. Later we unloaded the car and ate fruit and sipped wine and carefully in the evening made a fire. It was no surprise to either of us but felt like the natural course of things when that night for the first time we made love. It was not exactly an act of desire but rather of confirmation. And it rocked the both of us. It rocked us like neither of us had expected. My voices were all silent.

In the dead of that night Jacob got out of bed and set up his easel in the wide main room. The great windows flooded the room with moonlight, more than enough to paint by. Up behind him I crept. There for a while stood observing. And he was ignorant of my presence as his hands moved over the canvas. So strange, I thought, the forms of this life. Interrogated by reason they are inscrutable. Why should a man painting by moonlight in the wild backcountry of his civilization be of any real significance at all? Why should his painting? Why should a woman devote herself to such a man? It seemed to me as I watched Jacob that the answers to those questions would be obscure beyond all hope in the absence of guiding voices. How helpless are the children of the earth who have no voices to guide them. They are freer than me perhaps but compassless and with so few years given them in the span of a life to sort out where they must go and what they must do. My voices made perfectly explicit to me what was worthy of my deepest devotion. How many souls can count themselves so lucky?

III.

The summer when I was 28, I took a week of sick leave from my job at the Jewish community centre and bought a plane ticket to Victoria. I was a little more than five months pregnant with David. My husband gave me his reluctant, anxious blessing and asked if I'd like him to come along. No, I said, stay here for me: be my beacon from home. I might need one.

The morning of my departure, before I left for the airport to catch my early flight, I slipped back into our bedroom to kiss his sleeping face and found him in prayer at the window, *tallit* and *tefillin* wrapped around him. *Shema Yisrael Adonai Eloheinu Adonai Ehad*. Hear, Israel, the Lord is our God, The Lord is One. I unwrapped the black *tefillin* cords from his arms, traced with my fingertips the dark hairs that rose from beneath the leather.

He crouched and rested his head on my belly. Listening.

"I hope you find what you're looking for."

I hadn't flown since I was a child. I'd been twelve the last time, a trip to New York City. My father had had a series of Wall Street meetings and, obliged to stay a week but with plenty of spare time, had decided to bring his family down, show my mother and me around, take us to the Empire State Building, Broadway shows, elegant restaurants on the Upper West Side. It had seemed to me such an adventure, such a privilege, though the photographic record of the week suggests I spent nearly every minute with my nose in a book. The experience of flying I'd found terrifying and liberating. This time I had the thought of Aaron and David to comfort me, though also to intensify my fear that the plane might crash. I had more than my life to lose.

A rush of relief upon landing. I rented a car, raced south towards the city, the day hot and bright. Impossible not to wonder if he'd once driven along this same route, observed these same evergreens. Fifteen years is nothing. Had the airport changed, the highway? Had he even flown from Vancouver or had he taken the ferry instead? Were his thoughts of what he was leaving or of what he was heading towards? I rolled down the windows, half-convinced myself I could taste the ocean in the air, sang a soft medley to the vagabond's grandson inside me.

When I arrived in Victoria, I headed straight to the Segno Gallery, a narrow storefront tucked between a dive bar and an antique shop. I hopped out of the car, peered through the gallery's windows. And there it was. Close enough to touch.

Proof of life.

Aaron's cousin had stumbled across it online. After years of therapy and grief, including my runaway act at sixteen, when I'd escaped to Vancouver to look for him and my mom had flown west to collect me and refused, so painfully, to be angry—after all those years of resolving to forget my father, to move on, my husband's cousin had found him by accident. An art student, at work on a research project about a collective of small galleries in Victoria, Yoni had called me up and said: Man, you've gotta see this ... some dude on the other side of the country has painted you.

An astonishing resemblance. The portrait was on the gallery's website. He'd painted me at fifteen or so, an extrapolation of the girl I'd been when he'd known me. *Jacob Belinsky*—the name he was born with. I didn't tell my mother, who'd since remarried. I didn't want to reopen what I knew she'd still feel as a wound. But for me it was too late.

He has me seated in a giant rocking chair. My hands are folded in my lap. Behind me is a window that lights me; through it can be seen a dry and barren plain that stretches to the horizon, a landscape that has a stark noon beauty but nevertheless seems treacherous. The portrait evokes an inconsolable loneliness, though this loneliness doesn't seem to emanate from me. My eyes are bright. A hint of a smile plays at the corners of my mouth.

Jacob Belinsky. I couldn't understand it. In fifteen years I'd searched online for him hundreds, thousands of times, every variant of his name. Fruitless, always. For Yoni to stumble across him like this, so casually, was almost beyond belief. Was his reappearance considered, intentional? Was he calling out to me?

Of course I couldn't be sure that he was—but I became obsessed with the possibility. For reasons I can't explain but that consumed me from the moment I saw his portrait of me, I needed him to know of the life growing inside me. I needed him to see my adult face.

~

Miles of dense forest, an earthen blur. I rolled down the windows, let the breeze dry my sweat. All the details the Segno Gallery's owner had shared over e-mail looped inside me: a string of images, not quite real, sepia news footage from an alternate universe. My father comes into the Segno one day a little more than a year ago, a pile of canvases in the back of a pick-up truck. He's exhausted, dejected after a day of visits to the city's galleries, his hope almost gone that he'll find one willing to display his work for sale. Helen Koreeda, the curator, wants his paintings as soon as she sees them. He entrusts them to her and drives off, disappears down this green-walled highway I now speed along. And then what? The reel goes blank. Ms. Koreeda had told me he hadn't returned to her gallery since the day they'd met. She sent all correspondence to a post office box in a small coastal town about five hours northwest of Victoria.

It was evening by the time I got there. I deposited my luggage in my room at the inn near the edge of town and wandered out to what seemed to be the main drag. Once a sleepy fishing and logging region, tourism had enlivened this part of the coast: there were a handful of newish stores, restaurants, and bed and breakfasts that catered to the surfing crowd in particular. The locals seemed friendly. They met my glance, smiled at me and my belly. I strolled along a pier from which I gazed out at the untroubled, undisclosing water. The bank, the library, the liquor store—all housed in old clapboard buildings. Never in my life had I felt more urban, more a citizen of the concrete canyon, wilderness of taxicabs. So much of what I observed I had no name for: the local tree species, the relationship of the ocean to the land: not a "gulf", perhaps an "inlet"? And though there was hypnotic beauty here, the day's last light glimmering on the water, I was also struck by the drabness of this town in whose environs my father had perhaps spent years of his life, its fog of parochial constriction. I didn't want to stay long.

I bought a sandwich, balm for my cramps, from a little rundown diner and found the post office just before it closed for the night. It was a claustrophobic room that in a hundred years probably hadn't changed in any detail besides the introduction of florescent lights. The clerk, a woman around my age, eyed my belly. I told her I hoped to get in touch with the man who rented PO Box 59.

"59?" she repeated.

"That's the one."

"A man?" She checked her register. "I just started working here, but according to the record there's no man listed for that one. That box belongs to Patricia Bender."

"Who's that? You know her?"

She blushed. "Sorry, can't help you there."

I wandered back down the road to the diner, which was almost deserted. The waiter who'd taken my sandwich order, a tall, husky-voiced guy probably in his sixties, noticed me and approached. I asked if he knew where I might find Patricia Bender.

He became interested in one of his cuticles. "Oh, no. That family hasn't lived here for years. Moved to Victoria a long time ago."

"But she has a post office box here."

"Don't know anything about that."

My audition for the role of amateur detective had just started and already I felt worn down. Crampy again, my swollen feet aching, David doing calisthenics inside me, I bought some fruit and a granola bar and drifted down to the water's edge. Dusk was settling, the day's heat easing. I sat on the edge of a dock and peeled my orange. Boats' rigging clanked in the wind.

"Hey, miss."

I looked up from my orange. A boy no older than fifteen stood at the edge of the dock, his long blond hair tossed by the breeze in all directions, skinny arms poking out of a tank top.

"You back at Campbell next year?"

He looked at me as though he were sure he knew me.

"Sorry, I think you must have me confused with someone else."

"You weren't a substitute at Campbell once or twice last year? Grade Nine English?"

"Nope, not me." I thought I'd try my luck. "Maybe you can help me out. I'm looking for a painter named Jacob Belinsky, I was told he's spent some time around here. Ever heard of him?"

If he hesitated, it was for no longer than a fraction of a second.

"Don't think so."

"How about Patricia Bender?"

This time the hesitation was pronounced.

"Yeah," he said. "Of course."

"I think she knows the man I'm looking for."

He chewed his bottom lip. "Well, if you're asking.

No nice way to put it. The lady was a batshit crazy slut. Slept with anything that moved. Famous for it. They say she met some guy at the inn where she was working as a maid, some old guy with money, and he literally bought her as his personal whore and carted her off to a shack in the woods."

My heart hammered. "You shouldn't talk about people that way."

"Whatever. Everybody knows about those two. Sometimes kids go out to their house and egg it."

I tried to hide the jolt this gave me. "So you know where they live?"

"Everybody does."

"You mind showing me?"

I fished the map and a pen out of my shoulder bag and passed them to him. He glanced at the map, at me, and jotted a mark near a logging road outside of town.

"If you're not from around here," he said, "how'd you know her name? Who are you, anyway?"

"Old friend of the family."

It was like I'd cast a spell and turned him to stone. He stared at me. When at last he revivified, he backed away.

"Hey, hang on. What's wrong?"

But he was already hurrying off along the dock.

Bewildered and hopeful, in that order, I rose and walked back into town.

～

"I'll be home before you know it."

Phone pinned between shoulder and ear, my hair still wet from the inn's unenthusiastic shower, I transferred some essentials (maps, snacks) from my suitcase into my shoulder bag. I'd try to find my father tonight. I couldn't wait till morning, not when I had so little time to spend here.

"Just a week."

"I have it marked on my calendar," Aaron said. "Believe me."

"You're still angry."

"I was never angry. I just don't understand why this couldn't wait till after you deliver the astronaut."

"I'm not going to go into labour at five months, baby."

"You're putting yourself under a lot of strain."

"Yes. I know."

"Just be careful, okay?"

"I will. Promise."

I hurried out to the parking lot, tossed my shoulder bag into the passenger seat of my rental car, stole a bite of the pasta dinner I'd ordered from the inn's restaurant. As I drove out of town, the sky was beginning to grow dark.

It was star-speckled navy by the time I reached my exit from the highway. I turned onto a narrow dirt lane, pulled up to the shoulder and wolfed down my food, got back on the road. The mouth of the woods soon swallowed me, the trees' canopy nearly concealing the sky. I snapped on my high beams.

My thoughts circled what the boy by the harbour

had told me. Was that my father? A man who'd abandoned the most enviable of lives to shack up with a younger woman in a small town? What a joke. Nauseating. Yet maybe even nausea was an overreaction. I didn't know the man. Would any debauchery make his absence worse?

There was a part of me that didn't care what he'd done, simply wanted to hear him apologize and say he loved me. He'd loved me when I was a girl, I know it. Not enough, you might say. But sometimes love can see itself clearly only with absence, with the passage of time. Sometimes love can know itself only as regret.

Absorbed in this fantasy, I'd probably been lost for fifteen minutes before I realized it and panicked. I hit the brakes; the car squealed to a stop. I peered at the uniform black woods around me. How far would I have to drive before I found an inn or motel? How much gas did I have left? What if I drove for hours in search of a bed and was left without enough gas to get the car back to town?

I parked well off the road, checked the locks eight times.

~

In the morning it wasn't long before I found the place I was looking for.

Deeper into thickening woods and then a clearing. Sunlight. At the end of a dirt road, a squat cottage. I stopped the car as soon as I saw it, concerned that he'd hear the engine. That if he heard me he'd take fright and bolt like a hunted animal. How many times had I pictured this moment? I wished that Aaron were with me and then felt glad he wasn't. Of course I had to do this alone.

Car door clicked shut. Crunch of leaves underfoot. No other cars here, or none in sight. Birdsong in the trees, endless forest around the house. Maybe he'd been enraptured to discover this place. Had he bought it, or had he stumbled across it like a lost boy in a fairy tale? Had he settled in for good, resolved to end his days here? Would I bring my child here? Impossible. The house might've been made of gingerbread for all I believed in its reality. And yet. Sweat on my brow, along my sides, between my legs. My hands to my belly, instinctive. I climbed the rickety porch steps, crept to the door, and knocked.

Nothing. No sound of movement within. The woods around me still and indifferent. I waited. Knocked again. No response. Then, inside, footsteps. A creak of floorboards. I took a step back, composed myself; considered the skirt I was wearing, light and summery and not long, wondered whether it were the right attire for a reunion with your resurrected father, oh well, too late; prepared my face, not a smile but also not an anxious grimness that might make him think I'd grown into someone smileless. I considered what I might say to him when he appeared in the doorway — earnest acknowledgements, stoical grunts, stiff jokes — and when at last the door opened, after what felt like an hour and was probably a quarter of a minute, my mind went blank.

Not him.

A woman. She remained in the house, the door opened no more than a cautious crack. If this was Patricia Bender, she wasn't as I'd pictured her. Emaciated, her face pasty, the woman in front of me might've been in her forties — I intuited that she was, or not much older than that — but she could've passed for sixty. She radiated infirmity.

Her eyes narrowed. "Are you lost?"

"Patricia," said half my voice.

"Yes? Who are you?"

"I'm looking for Jacob Belinsky."

She opened the door a little wider. Stared.

"Hannah," she said, with an impossible glimmer of recognition.

My laugh was unnatural, strangled. "That's me."

Dark and humid, smell of mildew. It took my eyes a moment to adjust. We passed through a cramped foyer, firewood stacked against the wall, into a large room that seemed to take up most of the cottage. There I discovered the reason for the darkness: all the windows, their casings tall and wide, had been boarded up. Slivers of daylight snuck inside through gaps between plywood and window frame. The obstruction made the cottage feel like a crypt. Along the back wall of the main room was a basic kitchen — gas range, paint-stained steel sink, jarringly modern blender — with a pair of doors beside it. The rest of the room was occupied by rickety wooden furniture, flimsy lamps, and a couch with ripped flower-print upholstery, set too close to a fireplace. A few books were stacked on the kitchen table, the text on their spines illegible in the dimness. As my eyes adjusted, I noticed many other books scattered on the floor, in piles and singly. I also noticed, along each wall, an odd beige paneling, waist-high.

Canvases. Dozens of them, faced towards the walls.

"Would you like some tea?"

I shook my head. She crept across the room, with an unsteadiness that made me wonder if her eyesight were failing, and sat in a rocking chair by the fireplace, a thin cushion beneath her. The rustle of leaves whispered into the house.

"How did you recognize me?"

"He painted you."

She released a torrent of coughs into her forearm. When the fit passed, she looked up at me, eyes watery.

"He's dead. I'm sorry. I buried him myself behind the house."

I felt like laughing long and hard but thought she would be startled, so I didn't. Such relief. Incomprehensible—I'd longed to find him, I'd come all this way. And yet I felt a burden had been lifted from me.

"How long ago ..."

"Last year."

If I'd searched harder for him when I was a girl. If I hadn't made myself forget.

"And these canvases. His work."

"Yes."

"Would you please tell me about him?"

She didn't meet my eye. "He was a special man. I saw that from the start. And he was wounded when I met him. Deadened. He became whole again here. I was part of that. I helped him."

"Deadened ... how do you mean?"

She eased herself out of her chair. "It's difficult to talk about him."

I was so overwhelmed that I might've just nodded and left it at that, but then the rattle of the leaves was pierced by another sound: a car approaching.

She froze. My stomach churned, David kicked. The car drew close and stopped. Engine off. Car door clicked open, clunked shut. Heavy footsteps nearby, in the grass, on the creaky porch. The doorknob turned, the door swung open. Daylight flooded the house.

My father stood in the doorway.

I couldn't feel anything at first. Just stared. By now he was well past sixty, but he looked a decade younger than that. He'd lost none of his bearing; the white hair seemed hardly to age him. That hair, always thick and wavy, had grown long. My hands went to my belly.

"Hannah."

His voice hadn't changed. Neither had his way of looking at me, gentle and attentive. His mouth seemed different. Somehow more ready to laugh.

"Must've been a long trip," he said. "Are you hungry?"

I shook my head.

"Let's step outside."

Sunshine, birdsong. I trailed a few steps behind him, struck by the athletic confidence of his walk. Weathered blue jeans, an old plaid shirt, the back of his neck tanned deep brown. I was so angry with him, dumbstruck with anger. And so fascinated by who he had become.

He glanced back, his eyes lingering on my belly; I felt a hot blush spread through me.

We stopped at the edge of the woods, in the shade. Right on cue my eyes were full.

"What is this, Dad?" *Dad*. Muscle memory. "What are you doing here?"

He stared at his hands.

"Well, you're going to have a grandson. Thought you might like to know."

And I started to walk away. I had no idea what I was doing, but I sure was doing it.

"Hannah."

"What? *What?*" Birds thundered from one branch to another above me. "What's so important that you didn't need to tell me for fifteen years, when you could've *looked me up in the phonebook* ..."

I felt ridiculous. I was twelve years old again, upset about some domestic injustice, ready to barricade myself in my bedroom in protest. I had no experience of what it was to be an adult with my father.

"Please," he said.

"I don't understand why you hated us so much."

"I didn't hate you."

"You left."

He stared at the dirt. "It's complicated."

"Fuck off. Really. Being thirteen years old and realizing your dad's decided he doesn't give a shit about you anymore, *that's* complicated."

"You have every reason to be angry."

I laughed. I laughed with all of me.

"I never wanted to hurt you and your mother. I never regretted anything so much as that."

"Nobody forced you."

"No, nobody forced me."

The birdsong deepened the quiet of the clearing.

"She told me you'd died."

He blinked. "Trish."

"She buried you behind the house."

"She worries about my past catching up to us."

"Your past as in me and Mom?"

"She's unwell. She doesn't always know what's what."

I glanced at the cottage, its rotting boards and peeling paint. "Why are you living with a sick woman in the middle of the woods?"

"She refuses to leave."

Squirrels scampered in the trees. I shivered in the sunshine, drenched with sweat.

"How about I introduce you properly."

I followed him into the house. Furious. Elated.

"Why do you keep it so dark in here?"

"Patricia says it's better for her. It wasn't always this way. We boarded up the windows last year."

"Your father knows I'm not long for this world," came her thin voice from the next room. "So any alterations he makes for my sake are temporary."

"You're gloomy today." His affectionate tone unnerved me. "But we can turn on a light, can't we?"

She didn't respond. He tugged the chain of a yellowed lamp on a squat table; the room got very slightly brighter. He went to the stove, ignited the gas. "I think I'll make some omelettes. Any food restrictions?"

"Not firm ones. I usually keep kosher these days, though."

"Really."

"Yeah."

He glanced at Patricia, still seated in her rocking chair. "Trish. My daughter Hannah."

"We've met."

"What do you do out here?" I asked her. "What keeps you busy?"

"I ease the birth pangs of his work."

"And … when his birth pangs are all eased? Do you have work of your own?"

"I manage the household."

My dad chopped mushrooms, added them to a pan. "Has Isaac come back from the garden?"

"Not yet."

"Isaac?"

"Isaac is our son."

You'd think that would've knocked me off my feet. But, maybe because I'd just been confronted with so many extraordinary realities, maybe because the thought of my father and this woman raising a child in that lightless shack in the woods seemed so singularly crazy that it had to be true, I wasn't surprised. Flawless dream logic.

"How old is he?"

"Fourteen." He lowered the heat on the stove. "Will you keep an eye on the food for a moment while I get him?"

As he left the house, daylight poured inside and escaped again.

I leaned against the kitchen counter, prodded the eggs with a spatula, glanced at Patricia. She sat motionless, her eyes vacant.

"You have a son."

"Isaac was an accident."

Her voice was ice slipped down the back of my shirt.

"Lots of kids are. Then they arrive and you love them regardless. So I hear, anyway."

She was silent.

"I can't imagine living out here with a child," I went on. "So far from other people. Must be tricky for him to learn about the world."

"Your father has taught Isaac more than most people learn by the time they're your age. Our son has lacked nothing."

"Sure, all I meant—"

"He's lacked nothing."

I felt a throb of pure hostility towards her. It disturbed me. "My father tells me you're ill. I'm sorry."

"Your father's a genius, but he doesn't know how to keep his mouth shut."

"It must be hard to manage an illness out here."

"My needs are nothing."

The front door opened, daylight swept in, and my father entered with the wispy shape of a boy behind him. I realized Isaac and I had already met.

The kid from the harbour averted his eyes when he

saw me, busied himself with unloading the handful of vegetables he carried: cucumbers, onions, tomatoes.

"Isaac, meet Hannah," my father said.

"Hi." He didn't look up.

"He's heard lots about you. The way you were as a little girl, of course."

"So you've been honest about what happened."

"I don't want him to make the mistakes I made." He took the vegetables from his son's hands. "He can make his own mistakes."

"You're in high school?" I asked my newly minted half-brother, who gave the floor his undivided attention.

"Yeah."

"Out here or in town?"

"In town."

"How do you get there from here?"

"Dad."

My father rinsed cucumbers, sliced them. "Isaac was homeschooled until last year, when we exposed him to the horrors of high school. He's since become a monster."

"Is that true? Are you a monster?"

"I dunno."

With disconcerting ordinariness, we sat around the kitchen table for lunch. My father had made mushroom omelettes and salad; I ate with great appetite. When I'd finished, I watched the rest of them eat in silence. I felt I was observing a family whose practices I was ill-equipped to comprehend, products of another culture, a distant age. Yet this was my family.

I caught my dad staring at my wedding band.

"His name is Aaron."

"And he ... keeps kosher too?"

"Yeah. Sort of. It's a work in progress."

"How do you mean?"

I fiddled with my fork. Not convinced he had any right to know about my life. "We both grew up completely secular, and we both felt there was something not quite satisfying about that, so we ... looked into it."

"I went to church as a girl," Patricia said. "Terrible. Everyone there to pass judgment and mark their place in the community."

"I think a lot of what drew me and Aaron to Judaism was a craving for community. We've made many friends through our synagogue. I feel much less isolated than I used to."

Isaac looked up at me. When our glances met, he averted his eyes.

"I'm happy you've found something in Judaism," my dad said. "Certainly more than I ever did."

"Would you like help with the dishes?"

"Don't be silly, you're our guest. Isaac, will you show Hannah the garden?"

Isaac rose, brought our plates to the sink, rinsed them. A dutiful, conscientious son. Raised in the wild like an animal or a god. Who, when asked about his parents by a stranger, mentioned no relation to the man who was his father and the woman who was his mother, instead described them as degenerates. I was fascinated by him.

He led me from the house through a small bedroom. A worn double mattress, tangled sheets, an ancient night-stand. Clothes in a heap on the floor, books in piles.

"This is their bedroom?"

"Yeah."

"And where do you sleep?"

"Mine."

Steps from the house, the woods enveloped us. There was no path, and he weaved and darted ahead of me. Nervous that I might lose sight of him and be lost, I half-jogged to keep up.

A few minutes later he stopped.

"This is it."

When my father had said they had a garden, I guess it was my own metropolitan prejudice that had led me to picture the kind of plot you'd maintain as a hobby in your backyard. Their garden, if that's the word for it, was magnificent. A wide clearing, deciduous trees in dense ranks along the periphery, walls of green and brown; a stream. In the earth on either side of that stream, an aston-ishing variety of plants. Some bore fruits and vegetables: strawberries, raspberries, onions, tomatoes. Others burst with flowers.

To make this. To renounce the life he'd made, with great cruelty, at great cost, and to make this. Of course it didn't justify his behaviour, redeem him or the time I'd wasted, grieving and enraged, because of his betrayal. But I couldn't help but be moved. It all seemed so for-midable — the sophistication with which the garden was

arranged, the sheer extent of it, the mixture of plants cultivated for their utility with others that did no more than
affirm the genius of nature, its voluptuous consolations.

Isaac walked along the edge of the stream. "I've built
a basic irrigation and drainage system. My dad helped
me. It's been set up here for almost two years."

"You built an irrigation and drainage system when
you were twelve?"

"Twelve and a half. It's pretty simple. Low-tech. Just
a way of taking advantage of the stream here, directing
storm water."

I trailed behind him. Glancing at the soil on either
side of the stream, I noticed networks of ditches, furrows.
"A lot of your food comes from here?"

"Not animal products, obviously. Or grains. We're
not proper farmers. We do eat a lot of fruits and vegetables, though."

He skipped along. His comfort, his pride in this
place were unmistakable. They made him look older.

"Why did you lie to me about your parents?"

"I told you what people in town say about them.
Especially the guys at school."

"But you could've mentioned they happened to be
your mom and dad."

"I didn't know who you were."

Yet he'd recognized me eventually. "The painting."

"Huh?"

"You grew up with my face in the house."

He shrugged. "I was just like, whatever. If you wanted to visit, great. Anything for a little change."

"You're not happy out here."

"It's so fucked up. I never realized how fucked up it all is. I'm such a freak."

"Most people feel that way in high school."

"I have to get out of here. It'll kill me if I don't."

He said it without glibness.

"You don't even know," he went on. "Such a fairy tale life out here, right? My mom's hated me since the second she laid eyes on me. It's gotten even worse since she's been sicker. It's like she blames me."

The way his mother looked at him, didn't look at him. The caustic way she spoke about him. "How can she blame you?"

"All she cares about is Dad. Every minute I took away from her is a minute she didn't fulfill her sacred mission to serve him."

"Her sacred *what*?"

"She thinks he's like a prophet or something. It's totally fucking insane."

"He must be flattered."

"She's got this degenerative neuro disease. Doctors in Victoria think it causes her psychosis, but they don't really know. Dad's been so busy with her lately, since she got sicker. I know they'd both find it easier if I just wasn't around. So it's not even like totally selfish that I want to get out of here. It's for them, too."

I didn't know what to say to him. My responsible adult instinct was to talk him down, reassure him that at least one of his parents cared about him very much, that pretty soon he'd be old enough to make his own

decisions about where to live and what to do with his
life and could leave his parents' home, if he wanted to,
without much difficulty. My stronger instinct was to tell
the kid to run.

"Is your baby a boy or a girl?"

"Boy."

"And you've got a husband."

"Yeah. The two of you might get along."

"I don't get along with most people."

"Where would you want to go, if you left here?"

"Somewhere with millions of girls and a good library."

I laughed. "That place exists."

We spent the rest of the afternoon together in the
garden. I told him about Aaron and home, my work at the
Jewish community centre, the terror and exhilaration I'd
felt since I'd found out I was pregnant. He told me again
and again of his longing to get out of the woods, off the
Island, away from his mother. He didn't know what he
wanted to do with his life, but he felt the education our
dad had given him prepared him for anything.

We returned to the house just before dark.

"A nice spot, huh," my father said. "Most of tonight's
dinner comes from there."

With several antique lamps aglow, the house no longer felt quite so sinister. It was almost cozy.

"Stunning," I said, apropos of the garden, conscious
of how weird it was to compliment my father on anything. "How long have you been working on it?"

"I planted the first seeds the year Isaac was born. It's

actually a much simpler set-up than it seems. It was something to occupy myself with. I'm unemployed, you know."

"You're a famous painter," Isaac said.

"After fourteen years of painting here for myself, I brought a few to a gallery. I'm not exactly a fixture in the art world."

"Let's just say you're a famous painter, okay? That way we can pretend life here isn't totally shit."

"Fifteen years in the woods, just educating this one and growing a garden and painting. Of course Mom and I weren't enough for you. You were looking for Eden."

From the bedroom closest to the kitchen came a hacking cough.

"Obviously he found it," said Isaac.

~

The silence of the night was uncanny. The moon had disappeared behind clouds, so I couldn't see a thing when, after dinner, I stepped outside to call Aaron. I crept around the side of the house, guiding myself along the wall with my hands. My eyes adjusted a little and I could make out the tops of the trees, silhouetted against the sky. They fenced the clearing in, kept the world out.

"Do you smoke, Hannah?"

My father approached, a lit cigarette between his lips.

"Since when do you?"

"Little more than a year. Another bad habit of my youth I buried."

"Another?"

"I thought I'd gotten rid of the painting, too. Funny how everything eventually comes back. If I were a believer like you, I think I'd go for one of the Eastern faiths. Cycles. Reincarnation. That sounds about right. It seems to me that most people are reincarnated a few times over the course of even a single life."

"I never said I was a believer."

He slid to the ground beside me, leaned against the house's splintered slats. He met my eye with an intensity that startled me. "Did I interrupt you? Have you made your call?"

I shook my head. "So what's your plan now? Are you going to hide in the woods for the rest of your life?"

"It's clear she doesn't have much time left. Eventually I'll leave with Isaac."

"Does he know that?"

"We don't discuss his mother's condition. He leaves the room whenever I try to broach the subject. But I'd need to get out of here anyway, I'm running out of money. Isn't that ridiculous. Fifteen years and soon I'll need a job."

He stubbed out his cigarette.

"For a long time I thought I was giving him everything, everything he might need. Now I wake up in a sweat convinced I've failed him, Trish has damaged him. I live in constant terror that he'll run off. I'm sure he'll do it. I'll wake up one morning and the car will be missing, I'll find it parked at the bus station in town. Not a doubt in my mind. Just a question of when."

"Why him and not me." Selfish, maybe. But it was all I could think. "Why so terrible to lose him but not to lose me."

"It was terrible to lose you."

"Bullshit. It was your choice."

He didn't say anything. His face looked bloodless.

"I'm sure Mom wouldn't have minded if you'd bought an easel and paints, if that's what you needed. Why couldn't you let us in?"

The silence swelled to minutes.

"I think if I believed in God, I wouldn't paint. If I truly believed, my life would be enough. The other pieces of my life."

The wind whistled. He brushed his hair from his face.

"I paint to inch towards an understanding of ... something ultimate. But that's madness. What kind of fool tries to paint his way to an answer when he's sure no answer is possible? Why live for the mystery if there is no mystery? Why not just accept the pleasures of the world?"

He rolled the butt of his cigarette between his fingers.

"I didn't tell you and your mother about my painting because I didn't know about it then myself. My painting is the articulation of a question I suppressed very persuasively in those years. But for some people I think such questions might be permanent."

His frown deepened.

"Sorry. I'm keeping you from your call. Your husband must be worried."

I shook my head, but he'd begun to walk away already. The moon rode high. David rolled over inside me,

passing in his sleep from one dream to the next. Exhausted, I leaned against the house and called my husband.
He picked up on the first ring.

"My pilgrim."

"Guess what."

My hands shook so much I thought I'd drop the
phone.

"I found him."

~

Startled from sleep. Cold sweat, full body ache. Everywhere dark.

I sat up and the room spun. Aware that I had seven
or eight seconds at most before I threw up, I stumbled
into my father's tiny, mildewed bathroom. Afterwards, I
tried to be as quiet as possible, checked that the area was
spotless, washed my hands with the tap open no more
than a trickle. No sounds from the rest of the cottage.

I crept back to the couch, unsteady on my feet, still
nauseous.

Isaac watched me in the darkness.

I almost cried out, caught myself.

"Sorry. Didn't mean to startle. I heard you get up,
wanted to make sure everything was okay."

"Everything's fine. Thanks."

"I'll head back to bed then."

He didn't. He settled into a corner of the couch and
wrapped his long arms around my pillow, peered up at
me.

"My dad says you're staying."

"Not for too long."

Only after we'd finished dinner had it struck me that the sky was dark, my luggage back in town at the inn. And my last attempt to navigate the woods by night hadn't been a success.

He avoided my eye. "I was wondering if I could ask you something. If you could help me."

"Of course. Anything."

"So. So, I. Um. Don't know how to talk to girls."

Another wave of nausea hit me, probably unrelated to his remark. "There's no trick. It's just like talking to guys."

"No, I mean I actually don't know how. I didn't know a single girl until last year. Other than my mom, who obviously doesn't count. I'd seen girls in town but never had a conversation with them. So when I met girls at school, I just acted towards them like men do in books."

"Which books?" I was pretty concerned.

"Exactly. Books aren't consistent. I mean, I wasn't going around asking girls to touch my crotch or anything. I just told them the nice things I thought about them. And then asked if I could kiss them."

My concern was leavened with amusement. "Maybe I can give you some pointers."

"How did your husband win you over?"

"He was just himself. Kind, soulful. Funny. You've got all the same assets he has. You just need to find somebody who can appreciate them."

"Right, yeah," he said, with a peremptory nod. "And

so, like, what did your husband say when he first wanted to have sex with you?"

"Uh." Aaron had said, more or less, *Shall we?* The end—not quite the end—of a long third date. "Can't remember exactly. But we'd gone through some preliminaries first."

"Same here. I'd been in class with these girls for weeks before I told them how I felt."

"It's great that you're honest with them. You never know, maybe next year you'll be the school Casanova."

"Fuck no. All I want is one. One real love. I find that, I'll hold onto it for the rest of my life. I know what my dad was like when you knew him."

My stomach somersaulted. "What? What was he like?"

"I'm not going to be that way, swear to God."

He straightened my tangled sheets on the couch, fluffed my pillow.

"How long are you staying?"

"I don't fly home until Wednesday. I could stay almost till then."

"Promise?"

"Yeah."

"If you feel sick or you need anything, wake me."

I thanked him. He sprang from my sleeping place and hurried back to his own. I thought, for the first time: he sort of looks like me. The shape of his face, texture of his hair. Those big green eyes. I wondered if he'd had the same reaction when he'd spotted me in the harbour, if even before he'd recalled my portrait he'd sensed a kinship. If, seeing me, he'd felt for a moment less alone.

~

The sky was blue, the sunlight searing. We lazed in the garden's shade. I had with me a well-thumbed book by Abraham Joshua Heschel, the rabbi and theologian; Isaac had brought *Notes From Underground*.

"My dad gives me reading lists. I'm developing at an accelerated pace."

"What else has he gotten you to read?"

"Lots. All of Shakespeare. Plato, Homer. Emerson and Whitman. Henry Miller."

"Really? Henry Miller? How old were you when this happened?"

"Twelve?"

"I think that might be child abuse."

"Nah. I read Miller before I knew what the big deal was about cunts or cocks. It was just a story. Sort of boring, actually. I think he wanted me to be bored so I'd remember my boredom when I had to figure sex out later. Like maybe then I wouldn't go crazy imagining it was the best thing ever."

"He's a controversial guy, our father."

"He also pointed out the parts of Dante that show what some people think happens to you if you live like Henry Miller."

I laughed. "Do you believe that? You're blown around by terrible winds eternally for your sins of lust?"

"There's no reason why it couldn't be true. Although, like, there's also no reason why it *has* to be. My mother sort of believes it."

"Really. I thought she wasn't a fan of the church."

"She thinks there has to be some sort of other reality. Or else what's the point of her voices, you know? She thinks there has to be something after she dies to prove her life meant something."

And if in the meantime she's miserable to the person to whom she owes the greatest part of her care, the son she brought into the world, if she condemns him to a life of trying fruitlessly to piece together why he wasn't worthy of his parent: too bad. Her higher calling exempts her from any charge of mere cruelty. Tough luck to be born the mystic's child.

"What about you?" He twirled blades of grass, slipped them beneath his rolled up shirtsleeves, at ease. "You believe in all that afterlife stuff?"

"It isn't a huge part of Judaism. The tradition is more this-worldly, more about sanctifying the everyday. Did our dad never talk to you about it?"

"Nah, he's not religious. He hates that stuff."

And yet his life here was all reverence. This garden. His art. The love he had for his second family.

"What was he like when you knew him?"

"I remember I sensed his unhappiness pretty clearly at times. I never understood it. I'm not sure he did either."

"Yeah. Yeah, Dad's a strange one, huh? I mean he's nice and all, but he's pretty hard to get a read on. I never know what he's thinking."

"You must know how much he worries about you."

"Yeah, I dunno."

"He does. A lot."

"I'm going to read for a while, okay?"

~

The woods must have scrambled my sense of time, because it was only as sundown approached on the following evening that I realized it was Shabbat. I hadn't welcomed the Sabbath without Aaron in nearly three years. Every Friday evening in Toronto, he and I would walk to our little synagogue, *daven*, return home to eat a feast of a dinner, and spend the rest of the evening reading and fucking. The next morning we'd rise early and return to *shul*, after which we'd meet friends for Shabbat lunch, usually at the home of Dave and Julie Greenberg, a young couple like us: raised in secular Jewish families, not wholly reconciled to that inheritance, curious. Back at our apartment, the afternoon would again be spent in rites of sex and study, before the first stars appeared in the Saturday sky and the holiness of the day — so the story went — departed. For three years this discipline had been a deep and constant pleasure in my life. Strange that I should forego that pleasure to break bread with my reverent atheist of a father.

He laid out dinner, a vegetable lasagna. Patricia, bedridden since morning and seized by hacking fits, had gotten herself to the kitchen table and sat, rigid, next to Isaac.

I took a breath, told myself it didn't matter if they thought me pushy or foolish, and asked my father if he had any candles.

"Why?"

"It's Friday night."

He rose and rummaged under the sink, where he retrieved a book of matches, a candle, and a tarnished silver holder. He set the candle in front of me, lit it, and turned away.

I covered my eyes, sang the prayer. Since there was no wine on hand, I proceeded, according to tradition, to say *Kiddush* over the bread.

"Shabbat Shalom," I said.

"Shabbat Shalom," said Isaac. His parents stared at him.

"So what are you painting right now?" I asked my dad.

"Same as usual. What's on my mind."

"Which is?"

"I'll know when I've finished."

"Dad's been selling work like crazy."

"Isaac is my biggest fan. My second biggest."

He glanced at Patricia. She didn't acknowledge him.

"You must be proud that my dad's work is getting recognition."

She was silent.

"Patricia isn't thrilled that I sell my paintings."

"How many have you sold?"

"I'm not sure."

"A dozen," said Isaac.

"Be quiet," said his mother.

"Why can't he answer my question?"

"He wasn't asked."

"Isaac, how many paintings has your father sold?"

"A dozen."

Her chair scraped backwards. With the table as a support, she pushed herself to her feet, picked up her plate, and hobbled into the bedroom.

"Excuse me a moment," my father said.

Isaac stood, snatched our plates, brought them to the sink and scrubbed them, hard.

When my father emerged, he stepped outside to smoke. I trailed behind him. He stood on the porch and listened to the night with lupine attention.

"I'm sorry for the pain I caused you," he said.

The breath left my chest.

"How have you grown up to be so loving? Why don't you hate me?"

"Just the way I'm wired," I said, barely.

"You should lash out at me. Leave me."

"Don't tell me what to do, you lost that privilege."

His laugh was hoarse.

I took his hand. "Let's go be with your family. It's Shabbat."

~

Just after dawn, Patricia woke in terrible pain.

My father pretended to be calm and focused as he rooted through her supply of medications, his eyes squirrely with panic. I offered to help; he brushed me off. I stepped outside in time to see Isaac run into the woods. Not long afterwards, my father burst onto the porch and, with a soft voice and wild eyes, asked me to get his son, put him in the car with me, and drive into town as fast as I could to fill a prescription.

I found Isaac reading in the garden, told him what his father had requested. At first he shocked me by resisting. Wanted to stay where he was. His muted revenge. Stepped on and neglected by his mother all his life, it wasn't that he hoped for her to suffer, he just didn't care to be involved in the scramble to relieve her pain. Finally I convinced him — said I wanted his company myself, which I did — and together we drove out of the woods, the morning damp and grey.

He directed me to the pharmacy in town. I parked and hurried out of the car, prescription in hand, and was about to head inside when I realized he wasn't following me.

"I'm gonna go to the library and use the Internet."

"Not now. Please."

"Just want to check something real quick. I'll be back before you're done."

I couldn't waste time arguing. The sound of Patricia's pain reverberated in my head.

In the tiny pharmacy, little more than a supply closet in a bungalow that also housed a doctor's office, I waited in line for ten minutes. When it was finally my turn, the woman behind the counter scrutinized Patricia's prescription with a zeal that struck me as judgmental. I tried to imagine what I'd say to my dad if his son slipped away on my watch. He'd insist he didn't blame me — nobody could stop Isaac if he were determined to run — but he also wouldn't know who else to blame, besides himself. Isaac must know what difficulties he'd create for me if he disappeared now, I thought. We're friends — surely he wouldn't choose such an awful moment for his escape. But when the pharmacist returned with the drugs, he was still nowhere to be seen.

I waited ten more minutes and began to drive around town in search of him. I parked by the harbour and scanned the decks of boats, dashed into surf shops and the bank and the supermarket to see if anyone had noticed him come in or pass by. No such luck. As I'd expected. He knew the town, knew I'd be looking for him, knew where he could hide. I couldn't linger with the drugs in my car and my father alone with Patricia, waiting. I'd have to come back for him.

As I entered the woods, the car's air conditioner on full blast, my phone vibrated on the passenger seat.

"Sorry. Need some time to think."

My gut leaped into my throat. "Where are you?"

"Don't worry, I'll call you later when I wanna come back."

"Wait, Isaac — "

He hung up. The little prick, I thought, dizzy with relief.

I rushed into the house, it sounded just like I remembered, or worse, or very much worse, my dad had lost all semblance of composure, he snatched the drugs from me and disappeared into the bedroom to administer them, and it was half an hour before he emerged and shut the door behind him and the house settled into a black silence.

Sweat-soaked, he asked: "Where's Isaac?"

I explained.

When I'd finished, he walked across the room and ripped away the boards nailed over the windows. They were thick boards; he flung them down like kindling. When all the windows had been revealed and the room was illuminated with a quality of daylight that was wonderful perhaps not only because it replaced the morbid dimness, he slid to the floor, spent.

"Much better," he said.

~

Shortly after two in the morning, my phone rang.

"I'm ready to come home now."

I sped through the woods, my high beams shocking the trees out of their sleep. My son twisted inside me. What was I still doing here? Why was I putting myself under all this strain? If something were to happen to the baby, I'd never forgive myself.

My brother crouched on the curb in front of the pharmacy, pale in the streetlights' glow. He looked so small and vulnerable that it took all my resolve to stay angry.

"Get in."

We drove in silence. He sat with his eyes closed.

"It's not that I don't understand," I said, as we entered the black tunnel of the woods. "But you've got to pick your moments better. He had enough to deal with."

"Wasn't about him."

"I need to leave soon, you know that. He won't have my help on days like today, he'll need you. You can make each other's lives easier right now."

He didn't speak for the rest of the drive.

The reunion between father and son was understated. My dad didn't chastise Isaac, just told him there were leftovers from dinner and his mother was in'less pain. Isaac hurried into his bedroom, and my dad went to check on Patricia for what he said would be five minutes.

An hour later he hadn't reappeared. I waited on the couch, stared at my reflection in the uncovered windows steeped in night. The house was still and silent apart from the occasional creak of wood.

David kicked. I had a cramp. And that cramp crested into another, and another, and my heart started to pound, and then the cramps subsided, thank God, but I thought, and it was like a slap to the face: I must be absolutely out of my mind.

I packed in a hurry. I left a note for my father on the kitchen table, slid another note under Isaac's bedroom door. And I slipped out of the house.

In an hour I was back on the highway, a knife's edge of the day's first light on the horizon. The rush of freedom, the relief were overwhelming. I was halfway to Victoria before this began to chill me.

IV.

The landlady raps at the door. Phone call for you last night, she says. Who, he asks. Claimed she was your daughter?

A charge leaps from his gut to the top of his scalp. What's the number. She gives it to him. Right away he calls. His daughter's husband's recorded voice asks him to leave a message. He says only hello, please call, I'm here. For an hour he waits for the phone to ring. It doesn't.

Claustrophobic, he slips out of the house and walks down to the beach. The early summer air is crisp. He stands, as usual, as is his routine, not far from where he stood when, nearly twenty years earlier, he looked out to sea and summoned the shapes of his life back east and found them evanescent. Here, before the tribunal of the mountains.

He remains in Vancouver because the hum of city life numbs him. That numbness he once sacrificed everything to escape has become a necessary salve. To live without his son, without knowing his son is safe and healthy, is impossible. He lives impossibly. Why can't he let him go? Because he's getting old? Because of his stiffening back, his weakening vision — his fear of dying alone? Or because his son is a necessary part of him: a tandem heart, an extension of his breath. Hannah grew up largely without him, without the best of him, but of Isaac's childhood he witnessed most of the waking minutes. He educated him. He taught him what he valued, what he doubted. His son's sense of beauty is his. And his son's laughter.

So goes the broken record of his late life, echoing inside him as he shuffles down the beach full of young people at the start of their lives, beginning their search or their denial of the search, waking to the mystery and living it in the blood or locking it securely in an airless vault to be opened after death. The scent of the sea rocks him. The mystery, he thinks, the old mystery, still there, still just out of sight. Reveal it. Reveal it now or let it not be revealed forever. I'm tired of waiting.

He paints for an hour when he gets back to his room, drinks more coffee, eats toast and fruit. Waits for the phone to ring. He paints a while longer. This, in his numbness, has become his life. He has no friends. He reads voraciously, half-convinced that some book exists, if only he can find it, that will lead him to his son. For similarly chimerical reasons, he frequents an Internet café a few streets over. Strangely, his recent painting, born of this benumbed shadow of a life, has met with a warm reception. There are now a handful of galleries on the west coast that display his work and sometimes even sell it. The income is helpful; when, on that last evening of his previous life, he walked into the bank and cashed half his liquid assets, he didn't expect he'd need to make the money last this long. Years ago, he would've been gratified by the attention his art's received. But his world without his son is a magic lantern show. Will I ever stop feeling guilty, he wonders. Will the day come when he'll seem to me like any other grown child, gone off to make his own life? Is my attachment unnatural, he wonders. As unnatural as once my detachment was? Why this anxiety when maybe he's thriving, happy? Why this fatal weight that never leaves me?

The phone rings as he puts his painting aside for lunch. Hannah's voice seems to him changed. Matured, more darkly melodious. Hannah, he says, all other words stunned into silence, the way they were when he first saw her grown into a woman, when she trespassed into his sanctuary and the pain of leaving, the consciousness of what he'd left, came flooding back. As it does now. With surprising ease, she says. I wasn't hiding. You're still painting? There's nothing else. His daughter is silent for a thickening moment. Before she speaks again, clouds pass and his room is filled with light of a fine dappled quality, ghosts of leaves speckled along the walls, his arms. I'm sorry I left the way I did, she says. I panicked. It wasn't fair. I've wanted to apologize for a long time. The absurdity of his daughter's contrition makes him feel sick. Please, he says. But when I tried to get in touch with you again, the woman at the gallery in Victoria said all her recent letters to you had been returned. I didn't know how to reach you. I wasn't reachable, he says. Your landlady tells me you're on your own now. Why don't you visit us? David's two. Come meet him. Stay with us for a while. I couldn't trouble you, he says. Don't be ridiculous, Dad. Family's family.

He protests for twenty minutes, but his relief when she doesn't relent makes him sob uncontrollably as soon as he hangs up the phone. Within a week he's packed up everything he owns, deposited a number of paintings at a gallery in Kitsilano for safekeeping, and gotten himself on a flight. He hasn't been on an airplane since his long ago journey west, and as the plane takes off he trembles, hands vised around the armrests, knuckles blanched. He calms when the plane reaches its cruising altitude, grows so relaxed that he almost drifts off to sleep. His mind leapfrogs between thoughts. How strange to return home so suddenly after so many years. To return, he thinks with a flicker of lancing grief, to the scene of the crime. Rebecca Weiss. He can hardly recall her face.

He dozes for a while, wakes shortly before landing, and becomes aware of a tidal pain at the edges of his perception. By the time he's off the plane it's overwhelmed him. As he wheels all his belongings in his carry-on, shuffles towards the concourse where his daughter awaits him, every nerve in his body radiates grief. He doesn't understand why he's still alive. He feels ancient. Pain crests into panic and his legs fail; he collapses against a wall in a hallway outside the concourse, struggles to make the breath go down. How has he wound up like this? Nothing left to desire, nothing to live for. What mystery, he thinks. The only mystery is by what means the world eviscerates you. Once that's revealed, there's no question left to be asked. All that remains to desire is oblivion.

It's in this frame of mind that he shuffles out to the arrivals hall, so it surprises him to feel—as he sees his daughter with her husband, a thin man with warm eyes, who holds their son, bright with young life and a full head of curly blond hair—a quickening of his blood he might almost mistake for joy. Hi Dad, says his daughter. And she wraps her arms around him. Her husband introduces himself, introduces his grandson. Flesh of his flesh. His grandson. Glad to meet you, he says, his voice and body unsteady. I'm Jake. Jake or Jacob, take your pick.

They drive into the city. He sits enveloped by his daughter's family, observes them in wonder, oscillates between excruciating grief and excruciating joy, terror

the base note. He feels like a child: helpless, aimless. I
haven't been to Toronto in almost twenty years, he tells
his grandson, whose eyes go wide. I have lots of wonderful memories of this city. Many of them involve your
mother when she was a young girl. His daughter's expression is both compassionate and wary. He under-
stands. I won't stay long, he says, asking permission to embrace the joy he feels by swearing his readiness to relin-
quish it. Stay as long as you like, says his daughter. David
needs all the Bubbies and Zaidies he can get, says her
husband from the driver's seat. That way he grows up
knowing who he is. He looks at his grandson, who's preoccupied with his own thumbs. I'm not sure I can tell him
who he is. Who are you, he asks the thumb-beguiled
boy. David, says David.

It's nearly midnight by the time they arrive at his
daughter and her husband's apartment, a two-bedroom
walk-up above a furniture store. He has no appetite, but
he accepts his daughter's offer of bagels and tea, afraid
that she might otherwise leave him on his own. He sits
with her in the kitchen as her husband puts their son to
bed. Unsure what to say; frightened that a too clear expression of the tenderness he feels, overtaking him tidal-
ly as his pain did, might alarm these young strangers
who are his closest living relations; alarmed himself at
his rending passions, his weakness, his inability to know
what he needs and what he lives for. Tell me if you don't
want me in your life, he says to his daughter as they wait
for the kettle to boil. Just tell me and I'll go, I don't
mind. She doesn't respond. The kettle boiled, she pours

tea, brings over the bagel she's toasted and buttered for
him, the cucumber she's sliced, and sits at his side. What's
left for me to do, he asks. I've lived a full life. Maybe it's
time to call it a day. We're always in need of babysitting
help, she says. You think you're allowed to quit this life
while Aaron and I can't afford to hire a nanny? Soon her
husband joins them, and they talk long into the night.
Mostly he listens. Picking his way forward along the
edge of a chasm, refusing to look down. Looking instead
at the faces in front of him.

He sleeps on their couch for now, a makeshift solu-
tion until they can figure something else out. He tends
to his grandson every weekday while the parents are at
work. The boy fascinates him, gives him great pleasure
to observe. They watch cartoons together. The boy dash-
es around the apartment, tyrannizes the furniture. There
are moments that evoke memories of his son's childhood,
and the pain is intense. But it passes. The boy doesn't let
him grieve for long, is too demanding, unforgiving of self-
absorption. He knows his babysitting regimen won't
satisfy him forever, his intellect will need more to keep it
occupied. But for now it's a respite. It occupies his time,
holds the emptiness at bay.

He considers calling his ex-wife but doesn't know
what he'd say. He could apologize, though the thought
of such a belated apology, its outrageous inadequacy,
makes him nauseous. He calls anyway. A man answers.
He hangs up at once. Later he calls again and gets her
machine, where he leaves a brief message. I'm in Toronto,
he says. I'm sorry to intrude. Just wanted to let you know

I'm here. Hannah tells me you've been well. I'm glad. I'm glad, he repeats, ancient history shuddering through him. Please don't call me back if it'll create difficulties for you. He hangs up, rushes outside, walks for hours. She never calls back.

One evening, he slips out of the apartment to buy basic art supplies. He brings them to the breakfast table the next day. What's this, his daughter asks. I have arcane wisdom to impart to your son, he says. When the parents have left, he sets up his easel in the centre of the living room, opens the blinds to let the grey day in. The boy observes him with uncharacteristic diffidence. Just a moment, he says. I'll show you. Everything set up, he leads the boy to the easel and stands him on a chair. Show me the world, he says. The boy looks at him, unsure what he's supposed to do. He guides the boy's brush to the paint, to the blank surface. Go on, he says.

The parents arrive home from work to find an alien snow of paint-streaked papers scattered across the hardwood floor. We'll clean it up, he calls from the bathroom, where he's scrubbing the boy's hands to try to dislodge the more stubborn patches of paint caked onto his nails. Over dinner he apprises the parents of the progress the boy has made, how their toddler has progressed from applying blobs of paint helter-skelter, with a primitive enthusiasm, to a subtler, more delicate approach whereby concentric circles are interpolated among the blobs. The parents, though sceptical, aren't uninterested. He is a painter, after all, and it may be somehow beneficial for their son to be exposed to the fine arts at a young age.

The next day, and then every day that week, he paints with his grandson. He continues to guide the boy's hand over the canvas, to suggest shapes he might make, patterns he might impose, intermittencies of colour that might produce a shiver of delight. Yet by the fifth day the boy clearly wishes to take charge. With a show of small-limbed resolve, the boy wrests possession of the paintbrush from his instructor. The hand that holds the brush moves with assurance. Slowly he becomes aware that his grandson is painting with reference to him. That at intervals the boy looks up to take him in. Comprehending, as if it were the most natural thing in the world, he moves to the window in front of the easel and sits on the ledge, in line with the boy's gaze. He observes his grandson, who still looks two-going-on-three, but two-going-on-three and focused. What does the little boy see when he scrutinizes the old man's face?

The boy drops his brush at once when his mother arrives home. He runs to her, throws his arms around her legs. As his daughter kisses his grandson, Jacob hobbles over to the easel, where, without looking at it, without even a glance, he folds up the portrait his grandson has made of him, goes to the window, opens it a crack, checks to make sure nobody's watching, and lets the paper fly out into the evening. The breeze takes it. Gone. He closes the window. How was your day together, his daughter asks, lifting his laughing grandson high in the air. Perfect, he says.

Acknowledgements

These stories were first drafted between 2005 and 2010.
Their early lives had the following highlights:

"Mine" won the CBC Short Story Prize
and appeared in Air Canada's *EnRoute Magazine*.

"Witness" received the Jack Hodgins Founders'
Award for Fiction from *The Malahat Review*,
where it first appeared.

"All That Flies From You" appeared in
Per Contra magazine.

"Sister" was recognized by *Glimmer Train*'s
Family Matters short story contest.

"The Baker's Apprentice" appeared in
The North American Review,
which nominated it for the Pushcart Prize.

"The Snake Crosses the Tracks at Midnight"
was published as an e-book by Found Press.

"Faithful" was recognized with the
Alta Lind Cook Prize and the
Norma Epstein National Literary Award.

~

Thanks to the editors and jurors.

Thanks also to Stephanie Sinclair, Samantha
Haywood, and the rest of the wonderful team
at Transatlantic Agency. And to Michael Mirolla
and Guernica Editions: class acts.

Thanks to the Canada Council for the Arts
and the Ontario Arts Council
for supporting my work on this book.

Thanks to my friends and colleagues who read
and responded to earlier versions of these stories:
Brooke Banning, Sofiia Rappe, Kevin Shea,
Anthony Furey, Melanie Leishman, Sigalit Hoffman,
Naomi Skwarna, Robyn Sarah, Marc Côté,
Jason Rotstein, Hrant Alianak, Aaron Rotenberg,
Adam Weissman, Nicolas Billon, Kathy Friedman,
Michael Redhill, Barbara Gowdy, David Bezmozgis,
and Al Moritz and my classmates in his
University of Toronto creative writing class.

Thanks to my family and to Kirah. I love you.

About the Author

Daniel Karasik has been a winner of the CBC Short Story Prize, the Toronto Arts Foundation Emerging Artist Award, and *The Malahat Review*'s Jack Hodgins Founders' Award for Fiction. His previous books include *Hungry*, a poetry collection (Cormorant Books), and three volumes of plays: *Little Death* (BookThug), *The Remarkable Flight of Marnie McPhee* (Playwrights Canada Press), and *The Crossing Guard and In Full Light* (Playwrights Canada Press). His critical writing has appeared in *The Globe and Mail, National Post*, and *Partisan Magazine.* He can most often be found in Toronto.

MIX
Paper from
responsible sources
FSC® C100212

Printed in October 2017
by Gauvin Press,
Gatineau, Québec